WHISPERS OF ABADDON

A Horror Novella

John Reedburg

REEDBURG
BOOKS & MEDIA

ISBN-13: 9781736553572

Cover design by: Reedburg Books
Library of Congress Control Number: 2025908298
Printed in the United States of America

To no one: Thanks for believing in me.

Death is not the end, but a transition to a new plane of existence.

ANONYMOUS

CONTENTS

CHAPTER 1

AMALIE'S LITTLE SECRET

Amalie arranged her dolls in a circle on the floor with glass eyes reflecting candlelight. Instead of her usual games, she had them pretend to explore the sea. The raging storm intensified the moment's gravity, yet she stayed hidden amid the household's commotion. She enjoyed being unnoticed. Sitting close to her dolls, she hugged her knees and hummed a lullaby from her dreams, experiencing constant renewal. The room flickered between dark and light as the tempest worked its way through the sky, throwing shadows across the floor. Amalie edged closer to the candle, imagining it a torch guiding her dolls across an ocean floor. Sometimes, she gave each of them a turn to talk. Miss Clarabelle showed bravery, dismissing worry. Miss Lola agreed, but her voice was less certain. Little Pearl said nothing. She never did. Instead of following, she preferred to let them decide. She sensed their hushed conversation.

Outside, the wind battered the shutters, shaking the floor beneath her. Amalie hummed louder over the sound of the storm. The peace of her little world was a stark contrast to the chaotic storm raging outside.

The window shattered, cracking. An icy rain rushed in, scattering toys and snuffing the candle. Amalie sprang to her feet and ran to the window, straining against the gusts to pull it closed.

The wind whipped around her, tangled in her hair, like something living. It had almost pulled her outside when it slammed shut.

Amalie sat back down, wide-eyed in the dark, still listening to the strange whistle of the storm. Despite the drumming rain, the volume continued to increase. Within the house, the sound of rain, voices, and her mental tune echoed.

The floor creaked beneath her, so she nestled down to pick up the dolls and rescue them from their unfinished trip. She used the storm for a backdrop to her game, her little voice finding its way over the roar of the wind.

A crack of thunder split the night, and the window flew open again. This time, Amalie didn't rush to shut it. She saw it bang against the wall, tracing the ghostly stream of rain as it flooded the room. For a second, she almost caught it—a single sheet of paper as it floated down from the shadows. A single, readable mark marred its yellow, cracked surface. A single word. "Child." She held it tight, as though it might take off on its own again.

She wrapped herself around her knees, watching the candle gutter and fade, feeling tiny against the pulse of the storm.

Downstairs, she imagined bustling, cheerful rooms, their noises indiscernible to a small child. Instead of voices, though, the house creaked and sighed.

Amalie curled in a tight little ball as if she could hide from everything else in her room. If she squeezed her eyes tight enough and tried extra hard, she thought she could almost sense words mixed up in the storm's music.

Between gusts of wind and thunder, she detected them: voices, eager and hushed, too far away to matter. Beyond perception, almost invisible. Almost, but not quite. She tallied the bubbles, each a bright, isolated sphere.

More voices now, louder, so she almost knew who they belonged to. Could they muster the nerve to climb the stairs? She might even let them try her game.

Muffled steps up the stairs. Words. No one to listen to them.

A tiny sound of disappointment eluded her lips. She unfolded herself, lifting her head to meet whatever was headed her way.

Amalie slumped against the wall and caught her breath. She experienced giddiness from anticipation but held herself close, listened to the shadows, let the wind call her name.

Étienne ignored her, running back down.

She uncoiled herself and pushed herself upright, toes wet and chilled as she trudged to the window again. Her gaze followed him, slipping past the weathered wood of the porch to catch the street beyond.

In the storm's heartbeat, she fought to discern them, to pick up a single piece of what she wasn't supposed to know. But all she registered was the wind as it pulled her back inside.

Amalie kneeled at the window and observed the scene unfold. She was going to stay put, stay in her own neat circle with her own neat games.

As the engine roared to life and carried Renée away, Amalie's eyes grew wide. Étienne stayed on the porch; his head turned back inside. She remained unseen and unknown.

In a rush, she swept the floor clear and hurried down the hall, so eager to catch them off guard that she almost didn't notice her brother in his careful routine.

Mémé's room loomed large at the end of the passage, all shadows and mystery. Amalie stopped in the doorway, waiting to be noticed.

Étienne was there, back turned, talking to their frail, hunched grandmother. His voice was a funny mix of concern and pretend-brave. Even in her strange confusion, Big Mama clung tight to his hand.

"Étienne?" The dim hall muted her voice. She intended greater bravery.

Her brother turned, not startled, just annoyed to be interrupted.

"Étienne, did you—"

He was quick to answer. Too quick. The question remains unfinished. He squeezed Mémé's hand, then joined Amalie.

"But, but the storm," Amalie protested.

"It's just a big wind. That's all," Étienne said with a shrug that was way too big for him.

Amalie wished to share the paper, markings, and the child with him. However, he'd returned to Mémé's room. Already gone.

In the world of her games, something or someone protected and contented her. Breathless, she ran until everything was far away again. Her wide eyes met a strange reflection.

On the floor, she sat and rocked against the beat of the rain. The dolls were in a tight circle around her. Their game, beneath the waves, surpassed Étienne's deepest, boldest dives.

The strange lullaby's words drifted through Amalie's thoughts. This time, she listened as she should. This time, she detected the noise.

Child.

Two worlds.

Voices like windswept pieces of paper.

When Amalie closed the window, silence fell.

Alone again, she was as she had planned. She feigned belief. Alone, she was playing. She didn't mind. She'd return to her game, to what she liked best.

The furious sky unleashed its wrath in a breathtaking display of power. Too big for even Étienne to deny his fear. But it didn't scare Amalie. She let it hum through her head, reverberate around the dark room.

While gazing at the aged paper, a gentle and distant feeling pulled at her, surpassing the noise of the storm. As her eyes traced over the writing, she knew that someday soon, she'd have to show it to Étienne.

Or maybe she wouldn't.

Maybe she'd keep it all to herself.

Amalie tried the lullaby once more. She gave each doll a name and a turn, pretending they were underwater in their own little world. It pleased her, though not as expected.

The wind wailed past her window. As it poured down the street, spooling and tugging along its wild path, all the other houses appeared empty, shuttered up tight against the weather. At the end of the block, a mysterious shadow loomed, sending shivers down her spine.

A man. Just a black smudge at first, running headlong into the storm. She wondered if he would turn.

But he never did.

Instead, he ran the other way.

The word caught in the wind. Its presence was unforeseen. The word:

"Abaddon."

It reached her ears before she considered listening. She kept it all to herself, wove it into her secret games, the strange additional note to play.

As the storm took its breath, Amalie filled the room with her hum.

◆ ◆ ◆

The world stopped breathing for a moment. Amalie clung to Étienne, his shirt, his hand, everything he was supposed to be for her. Then the wind let go, left her dizzy with its absence. The sudden silence made her laugh. "Hear it, Étienne? It's like when the roller coaster stops, right at the very end." Her brother squeezed her hand. "I heard," he said. "It's nothing." He sounded brave, too brave. Like he was playing pretend. Amalie saw the fog paint the streets white, sneak through the gaps in the walls, curl up against the windows like it belonged. The rain continued falling, slow and secret, and the world shrank close as a held breath. They waited for it to start again, held on, noted the storm in themselves as everything slowed to a tiny, awful stillness.

They didn't move until the room started pressing in on them. Not until Amalie's fingers slipped from Étienne's and reached up to touch the damp glass, traced circles in the fog as it grew colder and colder. Her voice broke through the silence like a stone thrown into water. "It's quiet," she said. "You think Big Mama is quiet too?"

Étienne hesitated, appearing unsure about the accuracy of what he'd perceived. "She won't be when she wakes up." He still sounded so sure of himself, so big. Looking at him, she noticed the shadows under his eyes, the tension in his jaw. She was the only one to see him, and it made her uneasy inside. Her result may have been unexpected. Perhaps she desired a return; games offered safety, a respite from the world's closeness.

She opened her mouth, tried to get the words to go up her throat. Instead, the silence fell between them again, tangled with the rain. Amalie slipped her hand into Étienne's again, pulled him close as if she'd get left behind. "You think," she started, but didn't finish. Étienne's voice was tight as he wrapped it around her. "You're not scared, are you? It's nothing."

But it existed. Amalie recognized its significance. She sensed it in her chest, so immense it restricted her breathing. She kept her gaze on the window with wide eyes, holding so tight she almost pitied Étienne. Almost.

The silence got louder. The fog got thicker. They expected

disaster; a bright stillness preceding a burst, a dark moment before a dream's end. It's possible Renée will be back soon. It's possible she wouldn't. Amalie faced a dilemma: break the silence, or uncover their secrets?

Etienne moved away from her. Amalie tried to hold on to him, wanting him all for herself. He looked at her sideways, his eyes dark and knowing—too knowing—as if he feared her more than the storm. Amalie tried to smile and make him do the same but failed. He turned away towards the fog and rain and secrets outside. She hummed, softly at first, her own little song against the silence.

"Mémé said," Étienne said, cutting her short. "Mémé said it's not real. What's in the book? She said not to listen."

Amalie went stiff, as stiff as the words she tried to catch. She tried to keep smiling. The room breathed again. Her heart matched its beat—fast and uncertain.

The storm loomed, following a long wait. The rain made tiny ghosts as it poked against the glass, and the ghosts whispered as they fell. *They know. They know.* The walls didn't keep them out; they let them in, let them through. Let them paint their shapes in secret across the room. Amalie didn't see, didn't know, only felt how it washed over her, wrapped her in its sudden flood, left her and Étienne floating through it with just themselves to hold on to.

A light so bright she couldn't think. Couldn't breathe. Couldn't even see her own heart twist.

Then the dark was big again. She felt dwarfed by the world.

The wind outside picked up again, built like it never even stopped. It slipped through the tiny gaps in the house, blew Amalie's hair against her cheeks, made her eyes squint and sting. It swept against them, over them, through them.

The vast room seemed insurmountable to Amalie. She was aware of her own voice calling to Étienne from a distance, inquiring about his location. Her voice was faint.

The lightning popped and cracked, split the world open.

This time, she saw.

Étienne was blurry beside her, so she reached out, tried to keep him from falling, from getting washed away by the wind. His grip hadn't changed yet. Not close enough. Not safe enough. She observed his hand grow long, dark, and turn into a shadow of itself.

She didn't let go. Couldn't let go. Something held her tighter than ever before.

She squeezed it harder. The chill, slight thing enveloped her.

Her eyes became enormous as the storm. The thing, not her brother, was large.

The storm cleared her vision. She glimpsed her paper, her words, her child's hands. Two worlds intertwined. She noticed the empty room, its plain walls, and its secrets.

Then she saw him—the dark figure.

Lightning popped and cracked, split him wide and long.

Eyes were red and strange and bright. Teeth white and long and sharp.

A familiar form, present since before her earliest memories. That she had caught on the edge of her sight.

Amalie's voice was loud, but her head was louder. It hummed, so the sound shook the air, shook the space between the notes of lightning. Her heart pounded, then choked, silencing her like a storm's last gasp.

A long, black shape stretched.

It curled its mouth into a shape that stretched across the room. It smiled with sharp things.

Its voice was the strange music of the strange storm. "You hear it too?" it asked.

Amalie tried to squeeze her eyes closed, but they stayed

wide—wide and bright as two small windows.

"Hello, little sister," said the figure, growing closer than Amalie's small hands, closer than the strange words of the strange paper, closer than she ever imagined. "It's time we had a talk about our real family."

It laughed, muted as a held breath, dark as a held secret. Amalie saw the shadows turn and twist, their shapes projected across the room. She didn't know them. Not yet. She would.

The words soaked.

CHAPTER 2

ÉTIENNE'S UNEASE

Étienne squats on the old chair in the living room, counting the loops on the fraying armrest, watching his mother's frantic movements. She hovers like a hummingbird with no nest, muttering anxious prayers as she fills her purse with the bare essentials of panic. Car keys, worn wallet, a small bottle of red liquid he recognizes as a last-ditch attempt. Renée ignores him. "Stay put and watch Mémé," she orders, dismissing him with a wave. Then she is gone, an unfinished gust leaving the door swinging open and the air full of footsteps and unanswered questions. T-Bone's injury is severe. Étienne eyes the shadows in the empty hallway, flicks his gaze to the pale ghost in the bed, Mémé Celestine, motionless except for her lips, whispering jigsaw words that never quite fit together.

He squeezes the armrest, nails digging into its worn fabric. Everything had been operating. Too smooth. Étienne returned home from school to a typical day, with no mysteries or messes, but now everything was falling apart around him as usual. Renée's voice had been high-pitched, cutting through the air as soon as he'd walked in the door. "Buddy done called," she'd shouted. "Your daddy's hurt bad, Cher. Real bad."

She's zipping around the house now, grabbing the keys she'd

lost last week, the faded St. John's wort he'd seen on the shelf for months. She's a blur of nerves and hurried determination. His insides feel hollow as he watches her. He knows she wants to be there, holding T-Bone's hand in the white hospital room, the tubes, the wires, the beeping machines. Instead, she is stuck with him, stuck watching Mémé Celestine, always stuck between worlds and obligations.

Étienne sits frozen, every sound amplified by the blood rushing through his ears. "Can I come with?" he dares to ask, knowing what she'll say. He's experienced enough to expect the story's conclusion. She stops and turns for the first time, her eyes fixing on him with that mix of love and apology he hates.

"You're too young," she tells him, her voice softer but no less firm. She shakes her head, a silver-streaked line of finality. "Just stay here and keep an eye on your grandma." The words hang like an unwanted guest sitting between them. The brief look she gives him burns more than the words.

With a deep sigh, she steps into the thick New Orleans afternoon. The screen door slams but doesn't catch, swinging open like a breathless mouth. Étienne sits alone now, the faintest traces of her worried energy still humming in the air, T-Bone's condition pressing down like a storm about to burst. Spinal trauma, she'd said, leaving a lot of ifs and maybes behind. Too many.

His gaze jumps from the loose-swinging door to the hallway where the shadows watch him back. This isolation feels familiar; its effect on him, even more so. Unwanted. He's spent most of his ten years being "too young" for everything that mattered. Increased maturity heightened his desire for participation. Even if it meant news and harsh realities. Buddy warned him: T-Bone's injury was severe; he might never walk. He projects seriousness.

A creak from the old floorboards breaks his thoughts, the sound like a half-remembered warning. He turns to the thin bed against the far wall, the soft sheets, and the mound of silence beneath them. Big Mama lies there, part of the furniture with how little she moves. He suspects she's unaware of his presence. She occupies her own private world. He tries to avoid considering the tales he's heard. About her spells. About the things she said to Buddy before T-Bone got hurt.

Étienne swallows and watches the pale figure, the weight of her past, and the rumors that come with it. They sit heavy in his chest, a mix of fear and anger and that odd sensation he sometimes experiences when considering her, like she's the one who understands him best. Her face is visible beneath the dimness, skin pale like the white sheets that engulf her slight frame. For a moment, he wonders if she has drifted away to wherever elderly individuals go in their state. Then he sees her lips move, cracking the air with a voice that sounds both lost and sure of itself.

"Water," she whispers, the word more than a sigh but filled with enough force to pull him from the chair. "So thirsty." She doesn't open her eyes, but Étienne knows she means it to him. Who else would it be for? No one else left. Only they, perhaps, Renée planned.

He navigates the room, sidestepping the spots he knows creak. From a chipped pitcher, he poured, observing her for clues. It's impossible to predict what he'll see in it. Some days it's a frail old woman, almost peaceful. Other days, it's something else, something that makes him remember stories he's trying to forget. He hesitates before bringing the water over, each step measured like a cat crossing into unknown territory.

Étienne sits on the edge of the bed and holds the glass to her lips. They move as she sips, enough to take a bit of water, and then she falls back into the pillows, deflated. He questions her awareness, whether she's oblivious to her surroundings, lost in her own thoughts. He almost wishes he could join her there. But the instant he has that idea, she startles him by speaking, her voice thin but clear, a note cutting through fog.

"You think I don't know," she says, a riddle wrapped in a warning. "You think I don't see?" She pauses, her breath like rustling paper. Étienne feels a chill climb his spine, the room's shadows deepening. He doesn't reply, doesn't dare. He hesitates, not from fear—well, slight fear—but uncertainty regarding her desires.

"Thought I forgot," she continues, the cryptic phrases strung together like ghost beads on a frayed string. "Thought I let go." Her blind eyes open, stare right through him, past him, into him. She surpasses all others he's known. He's unsettled and fascinated, therefore wanting access to what someone has kept from him. He doesn't like unpredictability and being left out;

"Stop," he blurts, almost more a command to himself than to her. "Stop talking like that." He has no desire to learn what she perceives. She avoids confronting her knowledge. His words, frail and inadequate, shattered. She lies back, her silence louder than anything she could have said. He can hear his own breath now, fast, echoing through the room as he sets the glass down.

The shadows settle back into their corners, heavy with unsaid things. He questions their awareness of T-Bone's impending fate. Perhaps they possess superior knowledge. The smell of Renée's leftover incense lingers, mingling with the weight of Mémé's unspoken words. Étienne sits in the middle of it all, wishing he could chase after Renée, but knowing he's got no choice but to wait, hoping that this time, he'll learn something worth knowing.

The room echoes with Renée's absence. Étienne stands, looks at Mémé Celestine's dim bed, and then to the corner where his sister arranges her dolls with steady hands. Amalie positions them in a deliberate circle, her voice a firm whisper. "I'm keeping the bad things away, Étienne." It sounds like a child's game, but there's something in it that prickles his skin. He observes her, split between wanting to accept her statements and the impact of his recent conversation with Mémé. He crept across the room, each footfall a monumental decision. The fading photographs and chipped furniture hold their breaths, bracing for the secrets they cannot keep much longer.

Mémé lies motionless, a piece of furniture herself, as Amalie keeps up her game. He thinks she's sincere. Not really. Her pale face mirrored the determination she showed when building forts, clarifying that he was unwelcome. Like the days Buddy plays her protector, the same way Étienne aspires to be. Her small hands placed a frilly-dressed doll nearer the circle's edge. She sits back, pleased with her work, and looks at him, her eyes daring him to doubt.

"Gonna keep 'em out?" Étienne asks, trying to seem unconcerned but hating how she understands it all, comprehending aspects that leave him bewildered. He questions her certainty, her composure. Amalie nods, her dark curls bouncing. "Gonna try," she says. There's a defiance to her words that makes Étienne swallow the rest of his questions. She is unfamiliar with T-Bone. Unaware this situation differs. Perhaps she's trying to rectify the situation.

Mémé's voice, a faint whisper, filled the room—words deemed lost. "Nothing you can do." Amalie scowls, not liking this interruption to her circle. Étienne knows how she feels. He shoots a glance at the figure in the bed. It surpasses mere competition. Everything is. Her puzzling words further confuse him, yet he remains silent, concealing his confusion from everyone.

He stoops, gathering his sister's stuffed toys, the ones with watchful eyes. A faded giraffe, a patchy bear. She makes a face but doesn't stop him. "Is Mama coming back?" Amalie asks, trying to sound tough, the way kids do when they are certain of the solution.

He shrugs. "Probably," he says, avoiding her eyes. "She gotta check on Daddy first." Étienne doesn't want her to conclude he's scared. Doesn't want her knowing he's not sure how much longer he can sit here without cracking like one of Buddy's cruel jokes.

"Tell her," Amalie starts, looking at Mémé now, like she expects her to chime in again. "Tell her the dolls are working." Étienne blinks, surprised she isn't putting up a fuss about being left. Maybe she's just like him, curious about what's gonna happen next and too scared to miss it.

He scoops up an armful of toys, nods to Amalie. "I'll tell her," he promises, wishing he knew more, wishing he could tell her everything is fine, will be fine, and having her accept it. Amalie turns back to her circle, pulling a stray bear in close, the way Renée had held them when they were babies. Buddy said they couldn't hold T-Bone now.

Étienne crosses the room, Amalie's unblinking eyes pricking him like tiny, sharp needles. He studies wall photos, worn furniture—family warmth, unspoken stories. They seem to hold their breaths, waiting to see what's going to unravel first. It's been a long, tangled day. A long, tangled life.

His steps are heavy as he carries the toys into the hallway. They thud to the floor, a messy pile of fluff and glassy eyes that don't flinch when he curses under his breath, the words Buddy taught him last summer. He stares at them, wondering if Amalie is right. If any of it will work. Perhaps negative impacts persist. Perhaps they desire closeness. Perhaps they desire companionship.

The hallway's shadows, dense and consuming, hinder his return to Amalie. He finds himself outside the small room they use as an office, the one with Mémé's old books and the box of herbs Renée brought from Rhode Island. She hasn't unpacked it all, too many fires to put out. Étienne believes she might grasp the idea that some issues are unsolvable, despite Mémé's one-of-a-kind remedy.

A breath catches in his throat, his heart racing like Renée's hands this afternoon. If Amalie remains calm, it could signify a closer relationship, increased advancement, or sufficient growth. Old enough. He received countless warnings: Don't touch the box; wait for instructions. It's all Renée talks about. Until they understand. What's up? Know who?

He shoves his hands in his pockets to keep them from picking through things that might be curses waiting to happen. His eyes run over the books, the small bottles and jars. They all carry the promise of danger and something even scarier. Something like possibility. The door groans on its hinges when he slips in, settling into the humid air and all its whispers. Étienne hesitates, a mix of nerves and eagerness, determined to show his maturity.

Mémé's breathy warnings claw at the back of his mind, each one a knot tying tighter and tighter. Thought I forgot. Thought I let go. He shuts the door hard, like that'll shut her up. Like it'll shut up everything he can't stop from wanting to know.

The hallway stretches, exceeding his memory; perhaps, it's the day's burden. Might be the weight of the years. He moves, toys forgotten behind him, Mémé and her scattered puzzles drawing him in. He's restless, the air restless with him. He's desperate to be part of it all. A desperate need to determine the culprit: one person, another, or something terrible. All the above.

When he reaches the room, Amalie looks up. "What took you so long?" she accuses, but there's more curiosity than complaint in her voice. Étienne gives a casual shrug, trying to play cool, trying to play at knowing more than he does. Striving to mimic Mémé's quirky remarks. "Keeping the bad things away," he echoes, pointing at the circle of dolls and the circle of his own roundabout thoughts.

Amalie accepts the explanation, turns her attention back to her army of stuffed protectors. "You think it's gonna work?" she asks, her voice soft and hopeful. Her question sends shivers through him, small as she is. She tackles core issues. He stares at her, feeling the edges of the room closing in, the edges of his confidence fraying. "I'm gonna try," Étienne says, repeating her earlier promise, but this time the words have a different weight. They're heavier, truer, more than just an answer to her. They're an answer to himself and all the thick, silent secrets that watch them.

He sits on the floor, picks up a loose doll, and adds it to her circle. They work side by side, their shared silence growing louder than all of Mémé's broken riddles.

CHAPTER 3

THE GHOST OF GEORGE BRUCKNER

The worn sofa gives a long creak as Étienne shifts his weight, anxious eyes darting from the shadows of the old house to the kitchen where his mother Renée and uncle talk over plates of half-eaten gumbo. He crouches low near the doorframe, trying to catch every word of their murmured conversation. They speak like they're worried ghosts might be listening. "Mémé's power was born from the forbidden gifts of Marie Laveau," Renée says, her voice shaky like the record needle that skims over the jazz tune in the background. Étienne swallows hard, the sound of his uncle's voice filling the silence. "That amulet she wears has always pointed to dark fortunes." An antique amulet on the shelf catches his eye, and he wonders if it's staring right at him. It's the first time he perceives the family's secrets hanging in the air.

Étienne tucks himself further behind the sofa's armrest, glancing every few seconds toward the amulet, its presence looming like a ghostly overseer. A vintage player leaks faint jazz notes into the room, creating an uneasy calm in the otherwise muted old house. Intensified voices emanate from the kitchen. Étienne strains to catch them through the thick New Orleans air, his skin prickling with the tension. He hears his mother's voice first. "Everyone was sure she'd never have children. Then all those babies." The words float to him, heavy with unsaid meanings. Étienne knows they're talking about Mémé again, about the secrets nobody else whispers about. Stir curiosity pulls him closer, almost against his will. He moves like a moth to light, inching until he's just out of their sight.

The air is thick around Étienne as he crouches low, smelling gumbo mixing with incense from the living room. "After George died, she lost everything," Renée continues, her voice dropping to a mournful hush. "You remember how Larson was born?" Étienne holds his breath, afraid even a single sound might give him away. His uncle answers, words so careful they seem measured by the ounce. "Wasn't three months after she got those books." Étienne's hands clench into fists. He's heard stories of George Bruckner, about how his ghost lingered in the family's new home. His pulse quickens as Renée sighs. "The whole town thought she lost her mind, going on like she did." Her words have a way of filling the spaces with ghosts of their own.

Étienne listens, each heartbeat louder than the last. He senses the entire room is shrinking down to that one conversation. Renée's voice shakes. "Mémé, did things nobody could explain? Doctors said it was a miracle when Larson survived." Étienne's eyes flick back to the shelf where the amulet rests, its surface gleaming in the dim light. A chilling mix of awe and fear holds him captive. He edges closer, every word pulling him in deeper. His uncle's tone shifts, turning as cautious as a tightrope walker's step. "She did more than anyone wanted to know about," he says. Étienne wonders if anyone includes his mother, or maybe even himself. The words are like steppingstones across a deep river.

The jazz tune hiccups and continues, an eerie soundtrack to the talk of secrets and magic. Étienne keeps listening, not caring if he's caught anymore. His mother's voice comes in a half-whisper, as if she's only now realizing the full weight of the story herself. "Marie Laveau gave her those gifts," Renée says, her voice the thinnest thread. Étienne stiffens, knowing this name well from hushed family tales and the snippets of gossip he overheard in Providence. His uncle lets out a breath like he's been holding it for a long time. "That amulet she wears has always pointed to dark fortunes." Étienne holds onto these words as if they're the last raft in a storm. They spin through his mind like leaves caught in a gust.

He hears chairs scrape against the kitchen floor and leaps. They're getting up now to check on him and his brother. Étienne bites his lip, the metallic tang anchoring him to his current location—too deep within an unknown realm. The next moment seems to last forever. Étienne is rigid with anticipation. He waits, wide-eyed and not daring to breathe, sure that any second they'll walk in and see him there. The thought should terrify him, but he's already too tangled in the web of their words to care.

Renée and his uncle sit back down, their conversation starting again in slow drips. Étienne's shoulders relax, but his attention focuses like the edge of a honed knife. "The things people said about that woman," Renée mutters. "The more they said, the worse things got." A chill overcomes Étienne as he considers the gossip surrounding his mother before their departure. He stares at the doorframe, his own memory flickering like an old film reel. His uncle sounds firm but far away, like he's the last voice before sleep. "I'm telling you, nothing comes from that kind of power." Étienne's heart skips, unsure if it agrees or not.

Renée sighs again, a softer sound, like she's lost in her own thoughts now. "She swore those gifts came from God, right until the end." Étienne imagines Mémé's face, so fierce even when they told her she was mistaken. He remembers her during one of her "bad spells," when she screamed at shadows only she could see. It had scared him almost as much as this conversation. Renée's voice cuts through, still holding that thread of doubt. "But they were anything but." His uncle picks up the thread. "I believe that more than ever," he says. His words resemble a final nail, something Étienne should hang his own beliefs on.

Étienne's thoughts are a tangled mess. He needs time, space, anything to let them settle into place. Renée speaks again. Her tone shifted; urgency, a burning fuse, now defines it. "We have to be careful. You know how strong it runs in the family." Étienne's breath hitches, wondering if she means the magic or just the trouble that follows it. He wants to hear every word, even as they push at the edges of what he can handle. "We can't let this happen again," she says. "Not to my children." Her voice cracks, and he imagines her eyes, big and dark like his own, full of things he can't yet name.

There's a long silence. The jazz record runs out, and the needle scratches at nothing. Étienne looks toward the kitchen, half-expecting them to come through the doorway. He waits until he's sure they're staying put. His head spins, but he knows what to do next.

He rises to his feet, believing he's grown in the last hour in more ways than one. He walks, his gaze fixed on the amulet. Its intricate carvings glint in the fading light, lines so fine they seem alive. Étienne senses this marks a mere commencement; a truth he avoids. He stands alone in the empty room, burdened by the weight of what he's learned to press in from every side.

Étienne wanders into the dim hallway, its walls lined with ancestors whose eyes watch his every step. The floorboards creak beneath him, a restless rhythm in time with his pulse. Their words follow him like ghosts. "Mémé's power was born from the forbidden gifts of Marie Laveau." "That amulet she wears has always pointed to dark fortunes." He stops in front of a cabinet where an amulet gleams like it knows he's coming. This one looks alive, each twist of metal daring him to reach for it.

The air is heavy with the smell of dust and old wood, making each breath feel slow and syrupy. Étienne can't dismiss the impression that he's intruding, a stranger in his own home, where even the walls keep secrets. The narrow space closes in on him with each step, the faces in the portraits looming larger, their eyes darker. They stare like they're daring him to learn what they already know. "Everyone was sure she'd never have children," he hears in his mind, Renée's voice curling into the corners of his memory. "You remember how Larson was born?" The words form a loop, tightening around his thoughts like a rope. Étienne moves forward, his feet dragging under the weight of all he doesn't yet understand.

He sees old trinkets and framed photos that suggest a complex past. Étienne's attention flits to a tattered doll on a shelf, its glassy eyes as unsettling as the ones in the portraits. They remind him of the many brothers and sisters he never knew. He's unsure whether the objects are relics or rubbish. "Wasn't three months after she got those books." That's what his uncle said, right before they talked about George and how the scandal ripped them apart. Étienne presses his hands against his temples as if to keep the thoughts from spilling over. Mémé's dark power, the family's shame, the miracles no one dared speak of—they all fill him with both dread and curiosity. He hesitates, thrilled that it's intended for him.

Étienne recalls the way the amulet caught the light in the living room, its presence as real as the questions it brought to life. He needs to know more. He needs to understand where he fits into this tangled web of secrets and legacies. The air grows thicker as he reaches the end of the hallway, his steps becoming faster, more urgent. "The whole town thought she lost her mind," Renée had said. "That amulet she wears has always pointed to dark fortunes." The words make him feel alive in a way that frightens him. A new determination takes hold. He knows he's closer than ever to something important. He senses a metallic tang. It's a sign that his life extends beyond this house.

He halts before a glass-fronted cabinet; anticipation crackles. Inside, an amulet rests on a velvet cushion, its polished surface reflecting a strange light. It seems different from the one he saw before, more vibrant, more dangerous. Each twist of metal and flash of gemstone looks like it holds a secret only he can uncover. Étienne hesitates, his hand reaching toward the glass but stopping just short. His uncle's warning echoes like a last plea for caution: "I'm telling you, nothing comes from that kind of power." His urgent needs overcome the words.

Étienne takes a breath, as if it might be his last normal one. He moves closer, letting his fingers hover above the cabinet latch. His mind floods with memories that feel too big to be his own. He sees Mémé as a young woman, clutching her forbidden books. He hears the murmurs of the church, the judgmental eyes of the town. He recalls her voice, sharp as a knife through the tales, declaring the whole thing a gift. Each recollection is a needle, pricking his conscience but failing to deflate his curiosity. He stands there, trembling with the force of everything he wants and fears to know.

The amulet pulsates; its presence both draws you in and repels. Étienne's hands shake, but he can't pull them back. A potent link exists; the amulet seems to summon him. He imagines taking it would be like holding lightning in a jar—beautiful, powerful, and deadly. "We can't let this happen again," Renée had said. "Not to my children." The memory should be enough to stop him, but it spurs him on. He wonders whether the warnings apply to him or if they reflect an older generation's fears. He breathes out, slow, unsteady.

Étienne hesitates, his fingers trembling just above the amulet. His wide eyes reflect the shiny metal, each twist and curl daring him to claim his place in this strange legacy. The surrounding hallway appears smaller now, closing in as if to keep him from leaving. A vise of tension gripped Étienne, paralyzing him with the weight of his decision. A boy, poised on life's edge, resembles a statue, facing something far exceeding his own scale. The silence is thick, stretching the moment into eternity.

His breath comes in quick, shallow bursts as he stands

there, the weight of his family's past pressing on him from every direction. Étienne can't escape the pull, the magnetic draw of what the amulet represents. Alone in the dim hallway, he senses the entire world has narrowed to this one choice, this single, unavoidable moment. His desire for power and understanding flares hot and bright, an undeniable force that overshadows even his deepest fears. Étienne's hand trembles in the air, his fate suspended like the breath he dares not release.

CHAPTER 4

THE STIRRING STORM

Étienne stands in the cramped living room of the New Orleans cottage as dusk settles; wind noises intensify outside while rain patters the windowpanes, and he glances toward the narrow staircase leading to Mémé's room where disjointed mutterings—a mix of muddled, confused phrases and sudden commanding intonations—echo. The lights flicker as the approaching storm casts restless shadows across the peeling wallpaper and creaking floorboards; Étienne's hands twitch and his eyes shift, emphasizing the observable tension as he steadies himself against the worn armchair. A persistent, low mumbling, growing louder at intervals, sets a palpable rhythm in the room that mirrors his nervous fidgeting; every gust of wind seems to herald further disarray, establishing the eerie backdrop for the unfolding evening.

The shadows stretch and shrink, creeping along the edges of the room, adding to Étienne's unease. The lights stutter once, twice, then dim, leaving the house in near darkness. Étienne runs his hand over the coarse fabric of the chair, then drops it to his side as he turns toward the windows, watching the rain race down the glass. Thunder rumbles in the distance, a low growl that vibrates through the walls. Étienne's breathing speeds up, matching the tempo of Mémé's persistent muttering. He flicks his gaze to the stairway, chewing on the inside of his cheek, and draws in a shaky breath.

Étienne takes a step toward the window, the floorboards groaning underfoot, as the storm strengthens outside. Mémé's room sounds, though softened by rain, cannot soothe him. She repeats a phrase over and over—a familiar pattern—then shifts into something sharp and clear. Étienne stops, turning back to face the stairs. Her voice dips low again, a soft drone against the steady beat of the storm, the unpredictability unnerving him. Étienne presses his hands to his ears for a moment, grimacing, before dropping them to his sides with a frustrated exhale.

He eyes the record player in the corner, an attempt at distraction, but the usual comfort it provides feels distant and unreachable tonight. The floor creaks beneath his sneakers as he walks toward it, slower this time, moving past the bright quilts draped over the faded sofa. Étienne glances again at the stairway. He can't avoid it—any of it—but he isn't sure how much longer he can wait. He stops at the record player, fingers hovering above the dusty records, before stepping back and scanning the rest of the room with an impatient frown.

Étienne mumbles to himself, words as nervous as his gestures. "Ain't nothing to be scared of," he mutters, though his voice wavers. To steady himself, he wipes his palms on his jeans, the rough cloth against his skin, and takes a few breaths. He repeats his attempt at reassurance, louder this time, as if volume alone might convince him. He forces a confident nod, throwing another look at the staircase, and stands straighter. The wind screams against the old house, and his moment of resolve slips. His gaze darts to the door, then the windows, searching for any distraction.

The wind carries distant sounds of music and laughter, ghostly and thin as they float through the churning storm, before the rain beats them back into silence. Étienne turns away from the window, smelling gumbo and incense wrapping around him.

It offsets the house's oppressive atmosphere and pervasive unease. He steps around the armchair, biting his lip as the strange voices upstairs rise and fall. The constant shifting from confusion to clarity is too familiar, and Étienne knows he won't be able to ignore it for long.

Dim light in the room flickered; wallpaper and his eyes played tricks. Étienne's hands twitch, his fingers curling into fists as he turns a full circle, growing more agitated with each rotation. The words loop in his head—nothing to fear—and he chokes on them when he halts and lets out a sharp, anxious breath. The stairway taunts him with its proximity, just a few steps away, and he squeezes his eyes shut. Étienne freezes, pivots, paces, seeking a solution before the storm and Mémé breaks him.

Étienne's shoes scuff against the floor, moving in erratic paths that cross the worn rug over and over. The sounds upstairs mesh with the angry wind and creaking house, a growing chaos he can't control. The unsettling mix keeps him from settling, and when he stops, he's out of breath. He flops onto the armchair, and the dust springs up around him. The lights stuttered with the loudest gusts and thunder, each flash revealing the room in a last flare.

He stretches his legs out, kicking at the air with agitated jerks of his foot, before leaning forward and burying his face in his hands. The air feels heavy, thicker and warmer than it should, but Étienne doesn't move. He remains seated, eyes closed, for a minute; the usual words from upstairs surround him. He's spent nights like this before, in other houses, other rooms. Each time, he promises he won't let it happen again. But it's different now, harder to escape here in New Orleans, where the neighbors remember and the whispers don't die. His frown deepens as he presses his palms to his face.

Étienne's lowered hands reveal a brief, sharp resolve. He can't ignore it anymore, can't ignore her anymore, not if he wants to know, and the frustration turns his movements quick. He heads straight for the stairs, where the shadows crouch and shift in the corners. A noise he can't quite identify comes from behind him, something between a crash and a wail. The storm? The voices? Étienne spins, holding his breath as he faces the room.

His eyes adjust to the changing light, which returns in uneven pulses as the shadows seem to retreat, collapsing in on themselves like they've lost their grip on the room. Étienne rechecks; windows, door, dusty records—potential hiding places —then moves. The low voices twist and blend with the howling wind, calling him upstairs to Mémé. They push and pull at him until he can't separate them anymore, until they are the same and he doesn't have a choice.

A sudden, sharp knock disrupts the fragile muted as Mr. Robichaux, the elderly neighbor with a weathered face and rumpled coat clinging to his slight frame, appears at the front door, seeking refuge from the swelling storm. Étienne hesitates before opening the door, and the visitor's gravelly voice breaks the silence with, "I need shelter from this storm," while his eyes dart around the dim interior. Mr. Robichaux's arrival results in a cascade of observable actions: he steps in, brushing droplets off his collar onto the scuffed rug, and exchanges brief, anxious but polite words with Étienne, whose frown deepens as he listens.

Étienne's mouth opens, a greeting or protest hovering on his lips, but the old man has already wedged himself inside. The door slams shut, rattling the narrow walls and adding to the chaos of storm sounds and flickering lights. "It's coming down out there," Étienne manages, voice taut as he closes the door and watches their soaked visitor shake the wet from his coat. The man, unawares, nods; his eyes dart around the dim space.

He grips the back of the armchair to steady himself, releasing it as if remembering he's a guest. "Thought I'd wait it out," Mr. Robichaux says, another set of knowing looks landing on Étienne. "Can't leave an old man out in this weather." Étienne hesitates before answering, shifting from foot to foot. He should experience remorse, perhaps, but does not. Not now. Not when he knows what's going on upstairs. He forces a nod instead, hoping it looks convincing, then points toward the chair. "You want to sit?"

Mr. Robichaux doesn't sit, not right away. He watches Étienne, the corners of his mouth pulling down into a suspicious frown. "Seems like it's gonna get worse before it gets better," he says, again casting his eyes across the room. His voice rises, gravelly and certain, as if he knows he's the center of attention even when he's not. "Bad time for the power to go out." Étienne shrugs, brushing a hand across his forehead, trying not to show how right he is. He follows the old man's line of sight as it travels from the worn furniture to the dusty records to the staircase, and his frown matches the visitor's as he listens.

The lights dip low, then lower. Étienne's patience flickers along with them, and it takes everything in him to keep his tone polite. "You want something to drink?" he asks, already inching toward the hallway. Mr. Robichaux lowers himself into the chair, water dripping onto the bright quilts and pooling around his feet. "Just need to dry off," he says. He pulls a crumpled handkerchief from his pocket and rubs at the back of his neck, not once breaking his steady, knowing gaze.

Étienne bites the inside of his cheek, forces another nod. He can still hear Mémé, her muddled phrases underscoring every second that passes. The lightbulb buzzes before surrendering, and the house sinks into an even dimmer state. He's already three steps away when Mr. Robichaux speaks again, voice echoing with too much confidence. "Never a quiet night here," the neighbor says, drawing the words out as he leans back. "Sounds like quite the ruckus."

The comment brings Étienne up short. He presses his lips together, tight, and gives a tense shrug before forcing himself to respond. "Ain't as loud as it seems," he says. The words sound thin, even to him, and he shuffles on his feet, desperate to distract the visitor. "Maybe you can tell me some more about your garden?" he tries. "When you're not—" He stops, gestures at the window, and shrugs again. Mr. Robichaux doesn't take the bait, though, just studies him with those watchful eyes.

The visitor glances toward the stairs, and Étienne tenses. "We could hear your grandma last night, too," Mr. Robichaux says, casual but insistent. "Right through the walls." Étienne opens his mouth, then closes it, unsure if he's more annoyed by the neighbor's persistence or impressed by it. The old man sits straighter, observing the effect his words have on the boy, watching as Étienne's attention stretches further and further until it threatens to snap.

Étienne has to look away. His eyes land on the muted forms outside, the lush shapes of magnolia trees flattening against the window as the storm pummels them. He watches the shadows dissolve, like everything else, and pushes his hands into his pockets to keep from shaking. The mumbling upstairs becomes louder, pressing down on him in ways Mr. Robichaux can't imagine. Étienne draws in a long, unsteady breath and turns to face the visitor again. "Must be the wind," he says, struggling to stay casual. "Makes everything sound worse than it is."

Étienne walks to the window, pretending to check the storm. He dawdles, eyes drifting back to the staircase, haunted by Robichaux's voice. "Not just the wind," the old man insists, grinning like they're sharing a joke Étienne doesn't know. "Too clear for that." His gaze flicks between the boy and the ceiling, daring a response.

Étienne drops his head, staring at his feet, and squeezes his eyes shut. "She does this sometimes," he says. The admission's torrent, rapid and erratic, reveals fresh ugliness with each word. He looks up, startled by the sound of his own voice, and sees the neighbor nodding. "It's nothing," Étienne adds, more firmly. He stands taller, holds Mr. Robichaux's eyes. "Mémé just does this sometimes."

It's hard to tell if the old man believes him. A long, silent moment passes, a silent war between them. Mémé's voice cuts through the stillness, rising in a sudden, clear phrase, and Étienne jumps. Mr. Robichaux doesn't. A hint of a smile, perhaps a taunt, played on his lips; Étienne swallows hard, noticing the strain, perceiving it, pulling him closer to the breaking point, and his remaining patience vanishes like rain on the window.

He backs toward the stairs, no longer caring if it's obvious, no longer caring if it's rude. His mind echoes with the words, "Can't leave an old man out in this weather," and the unsaid words come next. He's coming upstairs, Mémé, he's coming up. Despite the storm and voices crashing together, Mr. Robichaux remains still in the armchair as they overwhelm Étienne in unstoppable waves that he cannot avoid, neither now nor ever.

CHAPTER 5

STOLEN LULLABIES

In the dim light of the raging storm, Étienne enters Mémé Celestine's bedroom. He finds her lying still on the edge of the rumpled bed; the sheets are askew and a muted drizzle of rain seeps through an open window, adding to the eerie stillness. His eyes scan the room, noting the shadowy corners and the flicker of lightning that reveals the intricate patterns on the wallpaper. Hesitating at the doorway with a raised hand, his gaze fixes on Mémé's motionless face and the dull glint of the amulet resting against her chest, its surface unresponsive at this moment. Étienne steps forward, small hand trembling as he reaches out to test her cool skin. The shock is apparent in his eyes.

He shivers. A gust pushes the window further open. Cold air floods the room, making him step back and bump against the door. Clutching the doorknob to steady himself, he stares at Mémé. She's not moving and looks smaller, as if swallowed by blankets. The quilt's edge moves in the rain. Her hands folded on her chest with that still pendant resting on them remind him of someone he's seen in a coffin before. The house shifts with the force of the storm. He senses it on the floor under him. A lump forms in his throat that makes speaking difficult.

Releasing the doorknob, he gulped, entering; the floor groaned. He remembers Mémé's moan before her last evil spell;

everyone said how close she came then. Now she looks too muted, even with all the wind and rain outside. Blinking, he tries to see if shadows are playing tricks on him.

Thunder booms; the bedside lamp flickers, threatening extinction. Mémé's face is pale, and her white hair glows around it, like a saint's image from his storybook. She's just lying down. Only the storm matched his racing heart, mirroring the lightning's rhythm. He half expects to hear Buddy yell from his room, telling him to stop playing with the lights. Yet, only thunder and rain persist.

Tiptoeing toward the bed, Étienne wrinkles his nose at the thick smell of wet wood and Mémé's perfume clinging to him. The lamp flickers, lighting Mémé, the window, the floor, the heater. Shadows jump like they're trying to get out of the way. He's left alone with his breathing, the noise of rain, and that big, ugly amulet gleaming. He watches, awaiting its action. But nothing happens.

As he shuffled backward, his elbow struck a chair behind him. The sound seems to rush into all corners, but Mémé doesn't even flinch. He waits for her usual scolding, but it doesn't come. This time she is dead. He looks around, hoping someone will find him, but no one does. The air gets colder; a chill creeps through him, making his feet numb.

Mémé doesn't need the amulet anymore; it will be his now. Buddy will try to take it just like he took all his birthday toys last year. Buddy will say it's Étienne's fault he made her die just to have it.

Étienne's shoes are damp from when he ran through the garden and squelch when he steps. He stops and slips them off, his socks warm against the chilly floor. A shiver runs through him and he wraps his arms tight around his shoulders.

A single, wet hair clings to the tip of her nose. Her head lifts from the blankets. He recoils, thinking she'll shout, then sees its only wind from the open window stirring her.

He wasn't ready to say goodbye, not yet. His fingers hurt where they've curled into his shirt. Vision is blurring due to accumulating tears. He needs to tell them, unsure his voice will overcome the storm's din.

Étienne is shaking. He holds himself more closely; He closes his eyes and counts to three, telling himself it will be okay.

The storm swallowed the sound up, but a strange echo seems to linger. Étienne blinks, unsure where it came from. His lips press tight together as he turns away from the bed and makes for the door.

He stops. What if Mémé is only pretending? The old heater clunks; it sounds just like her raspy chuckle. Étienne hesitates, trying to decide what to do.

Étienne draws a long breath. He's shaking and can't stop. He leans in and stretches his hand out. The pendant hangs like a mean little eye watching him.

"Mémé is dead!"

He recoils at the volume, then flinches as his fingers graze her hand. It's colder than he imagined it would be. The intense cold shocks him; he believes he caused it, echoing Buddy's words. Étienne backs away, arms up as if to keep something terrible from grabbing him and dragging him under.

Étienne stumbles away. His fear seems confirmed. He turns and dashes for the door. His heart is racing. The rain sounds furious against the window. He can hear his feet and also feel them on the floor. Room noise fades, distant, trailing. One sound pierces through, loud and sudden, like a shock, and it makes him double his speed. His voice reverberated down the hallway.

"Mémé is dead!"

His shoes are by the door where he kicked them off. He stumbles, his uncooperative hands grasping for the handle. He pulls, hard. Nothing. He pulls again and perceives a small give. It's like trying to open a jar of old preserves. His fingers slip and it slams shut again, and he holds his breath and waits.

It appears once more. He didn't imagine it. A scuffle sounds nearby; someone's preparing an ambush. He is being watched.

Étienne listens for them to call his name, but the noise disappears, swallowed up by the storm. He found himself back at the beginning - isolated and imprisoned.

He recoils, supports himself against the wall, and recovers his breath. Rain pounds the window; he questions his vision's reality.

No one leaves that fast, do they? He wishes to shout.

He squeezes his eyes shut.

"No one."

That means Mémé did it. She left him for good, with nobody and nothing. He bites his lip and a noise escapes. It's one he's heard before, in hospitals and at church. A low whimper. This time, it's not someone else making it. The lump in his throat won't go away. It just gets bigger and bigger until it chokes out his other words and leaves only two:

"I'm afraid."

The sound reaches his own ears, but it must be loud enough for someone else. He senses it hanging in the air, on the brink of becoming a forthcoming answer.

Only this time, it seems different. It seems genuine.

Étienne snaps his eyes open and spins around.

He found it perplexing. The way it pulses, like it has a heartbeat of its own. It's glowing. A sickly, steady light. The room's hue: decay, death, the unnatural.

He's seen it that way before.

Once.

When she put it in his hands and dared him to try it on. She thought he wasn't old enough to remember, but he was. He recalls the past event, noting its near-replication in her current actions.

Killed him.

Mémé's chest rises and falls. Her eyes snap open and hungry and set on him. He's pinned in place.

It's her.

And it's not.

The mouth smiles, but the rest is all wrong…

"Alive and well, and under my supervision."

It's not Mémé's voice.

He spins around to see a tall figure standing in the frame, dark and looming like nothing he's ever seen…

"The famous amulet," the man says with a smile that doesn't reach his mouth. "I believe it has quite the story."

The same one Étienne just told…

"Ah. Don't worry," the man says with a gesture to the chair, as if it's the only thing holding Étienne up. "I've been observing for some time. This is not unexpected."

A gust of wind knocks the window all the way open, making Étienne jump…

His eyes dart back to the door. It feels distant, like the entire room did before the man's entrance. Mémé now appears ghostlike, far away and washed out. Everything is in reverse. His hands itch to reach for the handle again, but they remain still. His mouth, however, doesn't share their inertia.

"What are you going to do?" The question slips out before

he can restrain it, spurring a cascade of others that clog his throat. He remains perched on the chair while the house continues its creaking lament under the wind's weight. The amulet glows and observes him, mirroring Mémé's gaze.

Étienne waits in stiff silence. He has no other option now. None. He's outnumbered, cornered, and he can't decide which terrifies him more: the stranger or the possibility that the stranger mirrors Mémé. A secret exists, unknown to him, even Mémé. This thought sends his heart into a frenzy again. He imagines it might throb right out of his chest, and that the stranger might bear witness to it. He wonders if the stranger expects this spectacle or even desires it. A worse thought then occurs to him.

Maybe the stranger wants it to happen.

Étienne squirms in his seat, unable to suppress his discomfort. The questions persist, relentless as the storm battering against the house, filling up the room until it blurs the line between inside and outside, real and unreal. The longer it lasts, the more indistinguishable everything becomes.

CHAPTER 6

FLIGHT THROUGH THE COTTAGE

The howling storm outside cannot jockey with Étienne's pounding heart. Amalie's small hand is slick in his grip, her whispers drowned out by each crash of thunder. Her tiny feet pounded as they run from the horror that lurches behind them. Mémé's arms stretch out, a grim parody of an embrace. The floorboards creak beneath her relentless hunt. "Run, Amalie!" he shouts, his tone breaking with urgency. Muddy water splashes around them. A door bursts open, and Mr. Robichaux stands framed by shadows, armed with amulets and a tarnished crucifix. He shouts foreign words, flinging salt at the thing that was Mémé. The thing met each attack with a brutal, sweeping strike, flinging his body aside. The house's collective gasp mirrors Étienne's frantic search for an exit.

Amalie's frightened cries blend with the wind's wail, causing difficulty for Étienne to think. He drags her along, his grip tight. "We gotta keep going!" regardless of the burden. Thunder shakes the windows as they race down the hallway, past sagging walls and the faded portraits that seem to watch their frantic flight. Mémé looms closer, her blind pupils fixated on them. "Étienne!" Amalie whimpers, looking back, her pupils expanded with terror. He swallows hard, a tight knot in his throat. The air is thick, suffocating, like the entire house is closing in. "Don't look back, just run!" He pulls her, pushing himself to move faster, the old floors groaning under each desperate step.

A shadowed figure appears ahead, silhouetted by a flash of lightning. Mr. Robichaux, his expression set and grim, leaps into the hallway, holding out the crucifix like a shield. "This way, quick!" His tone was hurried. Étienne paused, his gaze shifting between the pursuing threat and the dubious help. Mr. Robichaux mutters strange words, throwing coarse salt that scatters across the room. It lands with little sound, lost in the clamor of their escape. Mémé keeps coming, a nightmare that won't stop. A terrible crack echoes through the hallway as she knocks Mr. Robichaux aside, his charms clattering to the floor. Immobilized, Étienne reacted to Amalie's pull, recalling the urgent need for breath and motion.

Amalie clings to his side, her breath ragged with panic as she slips. He holds her up, urging her to keep moving. "It's no use, Étienne!" she cries. He shakes his head, refusing to accept defeat. Mr. Robichaux struggles to his feet behind them, displaying unexpected determination. Étienne's mind races, considering escape routes—stairs, parlor, kitchen—but finding none promising. Water is everywhere now, muddy and hindering their escape. The water covering the floor makes running difficult. Étienne feels his own breath, too fast and shallow. Mémé's presence looms like a heavy, terrifying weight from all directions. He senses it, cold and unyielding, drawing closer with each labored step. Amalie stumbles once more, and he lifts her, pulling her with a strength he never knew he possessed.

Through the confusion and noise, Étienne remembers the far corner of the residence. His mind latches onto it, a desperate thought, a last chance. "We gotta get to the old storage room!" he shouts, almost to himself. Amalie is too tired, too scared to respond, but she keeps moving, trusting him without words. They wheeled, heading down another corridor, beyond drooping furniture and shadows that seem alive. Behind them, Mémé is silent and terrible, never slowing, never stopping. Etienne tightens his grip on Amalie, as if holding her could make it all less real. The floors creak because of the pursuit, each sound a cruel reminder that they can't outrun this. Étienne's vision darted in the narrow hall, soaked and gasping. He drags Amalie into the small, dark space, hope and anxiety tangling inside him. But as the tempest rages and the house shudders, he knows Mémé will find them soon enough.

Étienne can taste the fear on his lips, salty like the water soaking the floors. Trapped and breathless in the shadows, they crouch, their hearts pounding in their chests. His eyes dart to a loose floorboard, a hidden secret begging to be uncovered. "What is this?" His tone is a whisper, curious, scared. Amalie presses closer, watching with wide eyes as he pries it open. Aged letters, tied with string, bore a familiar crest. Their edges blur like the truth, waiting to be read. Étienne perceives wind and distant footsteps, but this discovery signifies something beyond exit.

Their breaths mix with the breeze's, a harmony of fear and urgency. The storm still rattles the windows, an angry, insistent force that appears both close and far. Amalie huddles closer, her face a picture of confusion and fright. "What did you find, Étienne?" Her tone is a thin thread in the storm's roar. The house creaks as if listening to their whispered panic, the walls pressing in on their small, shared space. He pulls the letters out, hands trembling. He stares at them, with unknown terror seeping into his bones. This is more than just running now. It's about knowing.

"Look, they're so old." Amalie's eyes are wide with a mix of fascination and dread. The letters, like ghosts, carry fragments of the past that haunt them in the present. Étienne holds them up, seeing how fragile they are, how easily they could fall apart. The embossed crest catches his eye, and the sensation is like a jolt to the system, a reminder of all he's tried to avoid. "This can't be," he murmurs, more to himself than to Amalie. But she hears him, her small body tense against his side, waiting for him to say what they both are thinking.

Étienne turns one letter over in his hands, the paper soft and faded, like it might crumble under the pressure of truth. "It's Grandma's," he declares, a weighty utterance escaping his lips. Family legacy: The crest matches those on old documents. Of Marie Laveau's legacy. Amalie shivers, whether from the cold or something else. He can't tell. "Are they magic?" she asks, the innocence of her question not hiding the fear behind it. Étienne doesn't answer right away. He looks at her, then back at the documents, his mind spinning with possibilities, with dread.

Intense wind prevents concentration; the internal and external storms are overwhelming. Étienne feels the letters' physical weight, intensifying the moment's danger. Though Mémé's steps fade, he senses danger. "I don't know," he admits, voice low and charged with everything he can't put into words. He spreads the letters, fanning them across the floor. Everyone a taunt, a promise, a threat. Amalie watches him, silent but questioning, a thousand fears running across her young face.

A strange calm washes over Étienne, the tempest's lull, a moment before everything comes apart. "There's more to this," he says, more certain now, though he doesn't know what he means. The words sound loud, even against the storm. The letters show blurred ink; a message remains to be deciphered. Amalie leans in, unable to tear her eyes away, curiosity and terror mingling as she tries to understand. Étienne doesn't know if he understands himself, but he's aware he can't let this go. Not now, not after all this.

"We have to read them," Étienne says, his voice firm despite the fear. This prospect frightens yet motivates him; Amalie nods, unsure but trusting him to lead the way. The wind screams around them, the house groans burdened by a hundred buried secrets, and the letters lie between them, yellowed and accusing. Étienne reaches for one, his hand steady now, ready to face whatever they uncover. He knows this isn't just about survival anymore. It's about the truth. It's about everything.

CHAPTER 7

THE KITCHEN CONFRONTATION

É tienne's heartbeat echoes through the kitchen, loud as a secondhand ticking down the end of the world. He doesn't remember running from the hallway, but his lungs burn with each gulp of air, and his arms are raw with red marks where her fingers almost closed. The walls crowd around him, jittering with shadows as if everything in the world wants a turn reaching him. His hand closes around the phone, his thumb hitting buttons without slowing down to look. There's a shuffling behind him, an insistent wheeze that isn't even trying to sneak up anymore. Étienne spins around, his arm crashing into the counter and his voice breaking into an uneven shriek.

The word sticks in his throat when he sees her.

Mémé Celestine stands by the door, solid and immense, filling the kitchen with a heaviness that steals Étienne's breath. Her eyes shine like two useless white beads in her face, but he swears he can feel them on him, sharp and alive, cutting off his escape.

"I see you, child," she mutters, the words sliding out of her in a sticky mess, and Étienne chokes on a sound that might have been a scream.

His back bumps against the wall as he pulls the phone to his chest, clutching it like it might grow teeth and snap him in half. It's cold and smooth in his hand, and the beeping of the dial tone is like a needle stabbing his ear. He blinks sweat out of his eyes and stares at the buttons, his mind blank and numb, like nothing he's doing makes sense.

Mémé shifts a step closer, the drag of her feet a slow and grinding scrape. It's a noise that claws its way under Étienne's skin, sets his heart to pounding so hard he's sure it will shatter in his chest.

"Who you callin', boy?" she asks, her voice rising with the crackle of old wood about to snap.

Étienne doesn't answer, can't answer, not with the panic squeezing his lungs shut. His thumb jams at the keypad, random numbers flashing on the little screen, each one just another punch to the gut.

"Better hang it up, less you wanna call him to me." Her laughter is a cruel and splintered thing, an awful rattling echo that vibrates off the walls and deep inside his skull.

Étienne shakes his head, uncertain what it's directed at— her, the words, or the overwhelming situation: a nightmarish house, and a suffocating confusion. Releasing his phone is like surrendering to an inescapable watery grave.

The phone slips in his sweaty grip, and he grabs at it with both hands, frantic and fumbling.

"Don't!" he cries, the word ragged and thin, but Mémé keeps moving, closer and closer, closing him in until he can't tell where she ends, and the shadows begin.

Étienne squeezes his eyes shut, his arm sweeping out in a blind, desperate arc. A momentary pause precedes a sudden, terrible event. His elbow hits the counter; a deafening crash follows. The immense iron pot of gumbo—weighing more than his head, overflowing—arcs, spinning, its steaming contents erupting like a fiery comet.

The spicy brown liquid slams into the ground in a thick wave, and Étienne is next, slipping and sprawling into the mess with the phone clattering out of his hands.

He blinks up from the floor, ears ringing and vision blurring with the heat. The amulet is on the little table right above his face, gleaming silver against the wood, and he sees the gumbo splatter before he hears it. The liquid hits the table with a sound like an enormous drop of rain, bouncing high and rolling across the metal in long, dragging rivulets.

There's an instant where it glows even brighter, the symbols shining with a vicious, electric light, and then it's like someone throws a switch. Everything just... fades.

The light dims, dulling down to a dirty gray. Étienne thinks he sees the shapes blur at the edges, fuzzy and soft like they aren't sure what they aspire to be.

He pictures Mémé's vacant expression. The light extinguished from her gaze, a mere shell of her former self. For the first time since they got to New Orleans, Étienne sees her hesitate, looks on as her enormous hands grope at nothing, grasping at thin air as she lurches against the wall.

It's only for a moment, but he knows what he sees. Her inner fire rekindled, burning fiercer, its survival intensifying its flames. Her eyes blaze, and her mouth pulls tight in a line that could break steel in half.

The phone lies between them, shrilling and helpless.

Étienne lunges for it, pushing through the tangled clumps of gumbo that slow his every move. The thick liquid is cooling, turning sticky as it tugs at his clothes, and his fingers reach the phone but skitter past, slippery and useless.

"Looks like you missed," Mémé breathes, her voice sharp as glass.

She doesn't rush. She doesn't have to. Étienne now understands her power: to manipulate, destroy, and create, even while motionless and silent.

He grips the phone; it feels like the solution to her persistent questions, perhaps his salvation if he can only understand it. He lifts it; however, it's lifeless. The screen goes dark, its single feeble blip the only funeral bell he'll ever get.

Étienne retreats, sliding on the wet floor, maximizing distance from her. She follows without moving, her will dragging him into her orbit, inescapable and relentless.

"Is that how you wanna play?" she asks, and there's an edge to her voice that makes him think she already knows.

The amulet sits on the table, smudged and hazy, the heat warping its perfect lines and staining them with the thick, greasy shine of fear. A change washes over Étienne, a potential chance, his eyes flitting between the amulet and Mémé.

His expression surpasses terror. Something reckless. Something that looks like hope.

"Then let's play," Étienne whispers, and it's like a match in a dark room, sparking up when he thought he was out of light.

Unspoken words lingered. They twist in Étienne's chest, tight and pulsing, ready to explode.

CHAPTER 8

AUNT YVETTE'S INTERVENTION

The old phone rattles once, twice, each shrill ring creeping through the crevices of the New Orleans cottage. Étienne lets it sit, glaring, daring him to answer. It's just him and the dust and the sun and the cicadas. He dismissed his fears. He answers on the third ring, his grip on the receiver revealing the pulse in his fingertips. Aunt Yvette's voice wades through the crackle. "Listen, Étienne," she says, the comfort like a whisper before a shout, the authority so certain it swells the room. "To control Mémé, you must speak the name Abaddon."

He draws a quick breath, pressing his face to the phone as though he can squeeze out the distance between New Orleans and Providence.

"Abaddon is Mémé's taken father," she explains, words like storm clouds as they settle around him. His mouth hangs open. His fingers drum against the armrest, against the uncanny dread, against beginning hope.

"My coven of good witches is standing with you," she says, and then a long sigh of static as she warns of dark forces and intervention. "Against the dark forces," she says again, the promise tumbling toward him, louder and louder, "that plague both New Orleans and Providence."

Étienne sinks into the couch, warm and lumpy under the glare of a reluctant sun. He peeks into the hallway, half expecting his older brother Buddy to appear out of nowhere, sneering about him being a chicken. But the house is empty, the corners stuffed with a kind of dusty silence that is too proximate. He shuts his eyes, hearing Buddy's taunts, their laughter brittle and fierce as they twist into his memory. The air in New Orleans is heavy, and it smothers him with its wide, watchful skies. Somewhere, a trumpet plays an off-kilter melody, a distant accompaniment to the clang of streetcars. Étienne presses his hands against his ears, only to be greeted by the creaking of the wooden floorboards and the faint, sinister rustle of wind through magnolias. His chest tightens, and he fights to breathe through the sensation. Mémé's shadow lurks everywhere, and her strange spells are like fingers around his neck.

A shrill sound fills the room, waking Étienne. He sees the old phone vibrating on the stand, its ring high and tinny. Different from the phones in Rhode Island, he considers it ancient, just like its owner. Étienne hesitates, eyeing the phone like one of Buddy's pranks, before grabbing it. Static crackles through the line as he answers.

"Hello? Is that you, Étienne?" A hum and crackle blend comprises the voice. It's Aunt Yvette. Her words, like whispers and screams, seep into the corners of the house. He hugs the receiver tighter, his heart pounding like a bass drum in a funeral march.

She doesn't wait for him to speak. "Listen, Étienne. To control Mémé, you must speak the name Abaddon."

Étienne's mouth went dry. He holds his breath, and he's sure Aunt Yvette can perceive it on the other end, without a hitch in the wires between New Orleans and Providence. He clutches the phone with sweaty palms, fingers trembling as he tries to catch every word.

"Abaddon is Mémé's taken father," she says, with a confidence that buoys him and a dread that sinks him all at once.

The room closes in. It echoes her command. Abaddon. Abaddon. The phone is hot against his ear.

Étienne tightens his grip on the receiver, aware of the rough grain of the old wood where it touches the couch fabric. The sound of her voice flutters through the house like something alive. It's overwhelming, and he can breathe. He loosens his hold and watches his own hand, as if it might belong to someone else, reaching toward something he can't quite see. He shakes his head, trying to focus.

Aunt Yvette's words continue. "The name holds the key to subduing her dangerous powers." Her instructions beat like a drum in his head. "Speak it loudly, with authority."

The world is spinning out around him. A jittery sensation skips across his chest.

"Be brave," Aunt Yvette says, her voice pulling tight and thin through the crackle. Étienne fights the urge to hang up and hide, to slip away from the phone's strange promises. He keeps listening, his jaw set and his eyes wide. Aunt Yvette's encouragement, though well-meaning, lacked the genuine conviction of Buddy's. It's different, but no less terrifying.

He straightens, biting his lip hard enough to sting. His heart crashes like cymbals in his ears. He wants to tell her everything— how the house is a ghost of itself, how Mémé looks right through him with those blind eyes, how even his own shadow feels like it belongs to someone else. But he stays muted, cradling the phone and bracing for what he knows will come next.

"You must use the name with all your might." The instruction is uncomplicated, yet it saturates the air with an otherworldly energy. "You must command her: lie down, be still." It lands like a curse, and the air grows thick, stifling. Aunt Yvette continues, weaving each word with purpose, leaving him breathless and empty at once.

Étienne leans forward, a soft moan escaping the old sofa as

it gives beneath him. His free hand beats a frantic rhythm on the armrest, fighting the rising anxiety that bursts in his throat. He fights the sound of his own fear, silent and tangible, reverberating through the hollow spaces inside him. Each beat of his fingers calls him back. "Abaddon. Be still." It transcends a simple promise or threat. That's the key. It has to be.

A shiver cut across Étienne's shoulders, breaking into his thoughts. He hunches lower, curling over his knees and pressing the receiver to his cheek. Aunt Yvette's voice stretches thin across the miles, but she doesn't stop. She keeps the words coming. They're hard, they're heavy. Like all the things he wished to avoid and all the things he must now face. Their desperation gives them cause for optimism.

The name, she tells him, holds a power too potent to lose. She says it again. She turns it into a prayer. It becomes a dare for her. Abaddon. He waits for it to seep into his skin, to become a part of him.

Unspoken words hang heavy on the call. The promise hangs in the air like a half-formed creature, hungry and raw.

"My coven of good witches is standing with you," she adds. Her insistence fills the room; the task's enormity expands as he listens. "We are with you against the dark forces," she says, her voice receding and then roaring back, the echo of every dream he's ever had, the answer to every question he can't bring himself to ask. It wraps him up and leaves him dizzy.

He pictures Aunt Yvette, her lined face and steady hands. He pictures her coven. Across the line, beneath a low, oppressive sky, winding roads conceal them; he remains distant, however hard he tries. "We are with you," she says again, making the words beat in time with his own panicked heart.

Étienne inhales, holding the air until it burns his lungs. The ultimate promise—of support, of kinship, of good against dark—sticks inside him.

His eyes widen at the uncanny authority in her voice. Her faith, as tangible as Mémé's dark presence, is almost more than he can bear. Knowledge and consequence fill her words. Her words are already becoming truth.

Étienne grips the phone. He grips the edge of the world. He's thirteen years old, and the universe is crashing into him with each electric beat of her warning, with every drum of his frantic fingers, with all the deafening silence as the line clicks off and leaves him gaping at the receiver in mute, astonished terror.

Like a caged bird, Étienne's heart pounded in his chest, filled with fear and a desperate urge for freedom. "Use the name Abaddon," Aunt Yvette repeats. Her words alter the room's size, reducing it to his slight frame. "Command her: lie down, be still." The instruction spins through him, seeping into every fiber like the heavy New Orleans air that pushes in from the open windows. Her voice boomed louder and more deliberately; the accented words cut through the static. "You must act now, Étienne."

His grip on the receiver is slack, and his fingers brush his face, tap-tap-tapping, like they might shake loose the clarity that the message demands. *It's there*, he thinks, beneath the noise, beneath the fear, beneath the sure sound of her insistence.

"My coven of good witches," she began again. The Providence wind caught her words, carrying them south, to him, like rushing blood, "is standing with you." A final promise—bright as hope, dense as dread—echoes over the wire. It burrows in deep and lands with such force he almost can't breathe. "We protect the light against the darkness," Aunt Yvette says, and then a long moment where all he can hear is his own heart, wild and loose and alone as the line goes dead.

The static swarms Étienne, sharp and insistent and loud as it bounces off the walls. He pushes his shoulder into the old couch, a soft thump-thump-thump that marks each desperate beat. He should say something. Anything. But the words are stuck behind the drone in his ears and the rise of Aunt Yvette's impossible promise. "Use the name Abaddon with all your might."

It tangles through his head, winding tight like the twist of cicada song and jazz in the humid streets, like the strands of memory that bind him to this house, this family, this fragile New Orleans world.

"Command her," she says again, the vowels heavy with authority and history and distance, "Lie down, be still." Her accented syllables clip through the long breath of static, through the long silence of him.

Étienne's fingers drum faster against the worn fabric, against the panic and the certainty and the sureness of her call. A breeze cuts through the room, spinning him in two different places at once. The smell of incense mingles with the chill of Providence, and Aunt Yvette's voice takes on an eerie clarity. "You must act now, Étienne," she tells him.

The noise recedes and returns like waves. The urgency floods him, drowning out all his thoughts, all his questions, all the tiny fractions of self he doesn't quite know how to put back together.

He curls around the phone, pulling his knees to his chest. His breath is shallow, his eyes wide. His lips part, and he thinks he hears himself say the name before she says it again. "Abaddon," he whispers. The word melts into the steady cadence of Aunt Yvette's instruction. It drips like sweat down his neck. This demand is inescapable. That's his sole remaining possession.

"You must be brave." Her words infused the space with the heat of New Orleans. Her words shattered his fear, and they are the most terrifying.

Étienne feels overwhelmed with dread, but as he receives simple commands, his mind calms down. He clutches the phone on the couch. His fingers trace a pattern on his face and the receiver, as if trying to steady his racing heart and hold off the surrounding chaos.

"I know you're there, Étienne," she says. "We are with you." Aunt Yvette's voice is like she's standing right in front of him, so loud and so close that he almost can't breathe. Her repetition pushes out everything else. It pushes out the memory of his brother. It pushes out the sound of Mémé's wheezy laughter as Buddy calls him a baby and she chuckles from her bed. Wherever she is, her blind eyes seek him out in every room. Fear yields; only her voice, his racing heart, and a delicate, sharp hope remain. The force of her words is as steady as the tick-tick of the old clock in the corner. It's a sound he's learned to live inside.

"You must not wait," she warns, her voice crackling like wood in the wind, "You must do it now." From Providence to New Orleans and right to the living room where he sits. Her confidence is a heavy load. Her firm insistence. The belief she holds. It's there, beneath the noise, beneath the fear, beneath the thick August air. It's there, he's sure of it. He just has to listen.

His hand is damp and cramping where it meets the receiver, but he doesn't dare let go. He won't let go. Not yet.

"Do you hear me, Étienne?" Aunt Yvette's words swell. Her words press against him until he is small and overwhelmed and nothing more than their echo.

The repetition, desperation, and urgency of his own fate whirl faster and faster through him, a vortex of emotion he can contain. It vibrates in the small hollow spaces that ache to be filled, hoping won't break him.

"We are standing with you." Her voice catches on the long sigh of static, on the promises she won't let slip away. "Use the name," she says, a command that is also a prayer. A dare. "You must do it now."

The rattle and hum of New Orleans and Providence, along

with his own shaking hands, trap Étienne. Her certainty is a solid, tangible thing. It envelops him. It reduces him to nothing more than the sure sound of her instructions and the blood in his ears and the crackle of the spells he's known his whole life. Her assurance grows louder and louder and louder, filling up all the empty places where Buddy's laugh used to be.

Aunt Yvette's voice echoed through Étienne, the room itself seeming to shrink.

It exists. He knows it's there. It's his, if he can just find it.

A final promise—louder than hope, louder than dread—shoots through the crackling wire. It's the only sound left. "We protect the light against the darkness," Aunt Yvette says, a declaration that sticks, a prayer that stays, a dare he can't ignore.

Next comes a moment that feels prolonged when the only thing he can hear is his own racing heart, uncontrolled and isolated, as the call disconnects.

CHAPTER 9

WIELDING THE NAME

In the dim corridor, Étienne tore the name from his throat. "Abaddon," he says, his voice raw with fear and wonder, and the surrounding air seems to bruise with the effort of it. Outside, the storm cracks and booms through half-open windows. Inside, his words crack and boom through the narrow hallway, each one setting loose an electric shiver in Mémé's frail body. The old woman's head twitches, and her face folds into a flinch that leaves her thin lips white. He says it again, pulling the dark syllables through his mouth, watching them crash against her old bones. The shadows seem to thicken as Amalie moves into them, standing with her brother as if her small presence could hold him up. Her fists are tight at her sides. Étienne repeats the word, shaking, shouting, wanting it to echo forever.

"Abaddon," he whispers at first, forcing the word out, its effect a tearing at the edges of his mind. Mémé shrinks, to no avail. He swallows hard and leans closer to her open door. Her old rocking chair sits muted in the storm's noise, the wood creaking under her weight. He says it again, stronger this time, tasting the heaviness of it in his mouth. "Abaddon!" The way her hands twitch with each attempt makes Étienne's heart quicken. She knows he's there. She has to. Her mouth hangs open like she's lost or afraid, and he pushes the word past his lips with force now, fighting against the terror in his throat.

The dim light trembles with each syllable. Étienne recalls his brother's taunts; "chicken," he'd been called, for shying from Mémé's room during its unsettling episodes. He's proving them all wrong. He has to. His eyes are wide and wet, his whole body trembling like the fragile windowpanes. Étienne remembers his mother's dismissive voice: "Boys, don't play near Grandma when she's not feeling well." She didn't know. None of them knew how strong he was, how he'd figure it all out without them. Étienne is almost crying now, but he won't stop. He can't stop. He perceives something odd inside himself, similar to a secret being disclosed.

"Abaddon." The name fills the hallway and pushes back against him, echoing in his ears. Mémé's reaction is fiercer this time. Her arms jerk, and her head whips to the side. He gasps at how hard it seems to hit her, a strange thrill working its way through his bones. Étienne watches her, each tiny movement, searching her lined face for signs of pain or recognition. Her stillness now constricts him. Étienne takes a step back, wiping his nose with his sleeve. The floor creaks beneath him like it's breathing. Everything seems too big, too dark. He takes another step away, ready to run.

Then he hears his brother's mocking voice in his head. "You're gonna let her win?" It sounds so real, so cruel. It makes him clench his teeth with rage. He's better than Buddy. Better than all of them. He takes a deep breath and is aware of the way his lungs strain. "Abaddon!" Étienne shouts, letting it rip from his throat with a fierceness that stings. Lightning flashes, and the world bleaches white around him for an instant, showing the tears on his cheeks, the fierce determination in his eyes.

His voice goes raw, and Étienne falls silent, catching his breath and listening to the howling storm outside. He watches Mémé's slight, unmoving form, the shadowed room. Something bothers him; it's like disappointment or doubt. Can he do this? Maybe he was mistaken. Perhaps his courage is less than expected.

Then Étienne sees her fingers tremble, beckoning him.

He closes his eyes and shouts the name again, the strongest yet, with the sound grating his throat and shattering the tense air. Mémé stiffens with a hard jerk, as if the word lands like a punch. Étienne bites his lip, the uncertainty clawing at him like a wild thing. He's doing it. He knows he is. So why is it so terrifying? He hesitates, gripping his shirt in small fists.

The shadows thicken as the storm closes in, drowning the house in noise. Étienne trembles like the window glass, taking another step closer. The room blurs, and he blinks hard. Everything will change. He senses it in the air. The words hurt him more than they hurt Mémé, he thinks. They make him shake, make him cry. He's proving it to himself more than to anyone. But he will. He has to. Étienne steels himself for another try, drawing a breath so deep it seems to squeeze his whole chest.

Amalie appears beside him. Étienne hadn't seen her move, didn't notice when she left the shadows to stand with him. She's silent and steady, and Étienne senses the warmth of her closeness before she even takes his hand. It startles him. He wipes his cheeks again, embarrassed at first. But the way she stands there, brave and sure, it gives Étienne something he didn't know he needed. His tears dry, and a wild grin splits his face.

"Abaddon!" he yells, his voice strong, with Amalie beside him. The power in it electrifies the hallway, a supernatural charge seeming to crackle through the air. Mémé spasms and gasps in her chair, eyes wide, taking each sound like a blow. Étienne's relentless repetition of the word escalates, growing louder and more forceful with each utterance. Amalie squeezes his hand as if in perfect time with him. Her eyes stay on Mémé, intense and waiting.

They are a team now, and Étienne knows it. It gives him power, more power than Buddy, more than any of them. He feels Mémé's secret magic humming all around him, alive and dangerous, and he's in the middle of it, making it his own. He doesn't stop, can't stop. "Abaddon. Abaddon." Each one is louder, more brutal. Each drains the old woman, each drains himself. Étienne's voice is hoarse but steady. His throat burns with the taste of it, but it only makes him shout harder. The air thickens with the effort and pain and wonder of it.

Mémé's final flinch sends her rocking back in the chair, arms rigid and shaking. The last syllable tears from Étienne like a release, and he collapses against the wall, breathless, laughing with disbelief. Amalie still has his hand in a tight grip. He squeezes back, dizzy with the heat of their success, the excitement, the awful magic of it all. The storm shudders with them, a last crack of lightning searing the scene in white, and Étienne meets Amalie's eyes, reading the same thrill and wonder and secret fear in them. More than words.

CHAPTER 10

TEMPORARY VICTORY

É tienne's nerves crackled like the static in the storm, the oppressive corridor squeezing him with its claustrophobic grip, while the musty scent of old books invaded his senses, gnawing at his composure. His mind searches for the right name and the right words. They leave his mouth, clear: "Abaddon." The hallway swells with them—an echo, a promise, a command. His pulse surges as he follows it up: "Lie down. Be still." Everything halts. His grandmother's troubled pacing. The old house groaning. The power of his voice matches the fear creeping under his skin, stunning the walls. Her silhouette freezes, blind eyes burning into him from across the space. Then something inside her snaps, and she turns, deliberate, away from him and into the darkness. A door creaks, and she's gone, swallowed by the bedroom and the shadows inside it. The house shivers in her absence, and Étienne shivers with it, his triumph already shifting into something darker and more burdensome.

Minutes earlier, the corridor had closed in on him, a ghostly maze pulsating with tension. He found himself in a corner where walls converged like secretive arms, struggling to project his voice. "Be still!" It left him weak and drained, a mere whisper in the heavy air. Yet, she continued to move. Shuffling, scratching, murmuring her half-sane words.

The candlelight dimmed and flickered, toying with his sight. Her footsteps thudded. His heart thudded louder. The words felt like stones stuck in his throat, the air thickening, enveloping him as she uttered his name in the darkness: "Étienne. Étienne, boy." The walls trembled with her feeble sounds. He stood there, anticipating a hold, exist the authority he once felt during Mr. Robichaux's glory days. Étienne's gaze locked onto her figure, wild and unsteady like a startled horse. How long until it overtook him?

She stood where the light failed. Her frame, her spirit, something larger and fiercer than her feeble old body should be. The power he couldn't hold. The word he couldn't say. He failed to grasp it. The others shouted it as they drove her through the hall. A thousand strange syllables, but only one that stopped her. A word with a shape like nothing else, searing itself into his brain. "Abaddon." Étienne pressed it past his lips, this time with less fear, this time with more control, savoring the way it stretched and curled inside his mouth. Mémé paused midstride, and he watched as that terrible presence seemed to coil and writhe beneath her. He gasped for breath, noticing the faint shadows in the narrow passage and hearing the old cottage groan. Growing stronger than before, he consumed them. Then, with all of him behind it, he shouted. "Lie down! Be still!"

That was when it happened. When he broke it. The air. Her pace. The unsteady drumming of his heart. Big Mama's whole body went rigid, its weight bearing down and collapsing inward. Her head turned. One jerky motion and her sightless eyes latched onto his. The intensity inside them washed over him, deep and molten, fixing Étienne to the floor with fear or fire or triumph. A desperate, almost human quality, in her mouth's sharp twist, fueled his hatred. It escaped before identification. Her form shrank. Her shadowed soul slipped back inside the fragile body that could hold it, and Mémé moved with purpose, as if she knew what she was doing. Slower than a storm, but faster than defeat. Her retreat scorched him with her blind eyes across the hall.

Turning, turning, turning, her silhouette lost its shape. Then, it vanished, leaving only house groans and a clicking door.

Étienne's thoughts went everywhere. He couldn't get them back. Many questions, insufficient time. The corridor, the rooms, and the intact house expanding to fill the shadows where she'd been. Perhaps even the entire city. Even the wind and the rain. Could she absorb a storm within herself, just as she had absorbed his empty words over the years? She'd gulped them down and turned them into poison, and now he spat them back. This was a start. One command. They might have traveled. It's possible he wouldn't have to escape next time. Perhaps next time — Étienne wasn't sure what followed. If he pondered it or if the ghost of it haunted the walls. He dwelt upon the external storm, a lengthy period. Minutes or hours. It didn't matter. She was inside, he was outside. One question consumed him: "What have I done?"

The old house swelled and sighed, blowing back his question and the stillness that carried it. His first actual words to her, and they weren't just sounds. Not anymore. Their dark, sturdy forms, equipped with limbs and powerful muscles, dominated the corridor. "Abaddon," he heard himself saying. A hundredth time, but also brand new. And she halted. Paused. He clung to that, and the fragile courage it gave him. This could be why George took him, the one she couldn't bully. Was it why she came here? And why they'd tried so hard to keep him from her? This power may have always belonged to him. Now that he'd said it, now that he'd done it, she couldn't have it. He thought of Mr. Robichaux and how fast he would run back to Providence. He almost smiled, then the weight of his victory crashed down on him. Étienne fought to hold it up, but it seeped into him and sank him deeper and deeper. The name. The command. The storm. Everything was dark and heavy and more than one boy could hold.

It washed over him until the sound of Mémé's steps faded, until the smell of her incense left his clothes. The rain spat through the open windows and splattered against the floor. Étienne slumped beside it, alone with the wild terror of her, alone with the shame and the joy of being alone. He stayed that way until everything vanished. That location felt unknown to them.

The shriek of the wind is louder than George's torn cry. Louder than the awful moment, Étienne's command struck them both. It pounds his ears, leaving no room for anything else, until the faint creak of a door forces its way into his thoughts. It's Mémé. Back already. Dark magic recoils from the sheer intensity of her will. He stiffens and waits for her figure to emerge from the swirling shadows.

Instead, another form, softer and more hesitant, cuts its shape against the dim hallway. Étienne exhales, relief and anger wrestling inside him as he looks at George's frail movements. His steps echo hers as he walks down the hall. He struggles to maintain control over a boy's voice linked to an old woman's spirit. He can't hold his ground or move beyond the armchair where he gave up after losing the advantage.

Étienne finds his breath and his voice, and for the first time, Mr. A tremor ran through Robichaux's body.

The thin, soft presence of him grows thicker and more real with each unsteady step. He moves, steadying himself on the furniture as he makes his way toward the living room door. The pale hand opening the door contrasts with the wood; he seems diminished, a faint outline. Mr. Robichaux flinches as the wind thrashes, shivering and alive, through the dim hallway. He pauses, waiting for another blast, another shout from the small boy's mouth. A distant ghost train whistle is the only sound disturbing the muted air. Étienne holds his breath. Across the hall, they exchanged a first-time glance. George's face is bright with relief and raw with pain. Beyond gray and white, its hues exceeded those staining his skin and the carpet when Big Mama's magic chilled it. His free hand has darkened. Drenched in a liquid that other adults would consider accidental if they saw it, unable to mention his name without shaking. Bandaged and angry, it hangs at his side like an old possession, unwanted and unimportant, while he drags himself forward.

Étienne lets out the breath he was holding. Now, he isn't the first to avoid eye contact. The boy's words move through the old house like his grandmother did, sinking into George and pulling him out the other side, patchy and worn. Their plan might involve this action, regardless of the extreme distance and intensity. Étienne half-expects him to scurry away. Instead, the strange, frail figure moves closer. Closer. Past the door. Into the hall. Étienne's heart skips a beat, and it pleases him to see the startled look on the older man's face, to know his words have left their mark. He stares George down with dark, bright eyes, unblinking and firm. He doesn't need to ask who's in control now. Mr. Robichaux stands there, unsure of himself, protecting it from storm and fear with steady hands. The small boy's unusual, confident tone puzzled me. Étienne doesn't give him a chance to answer the question he's not brave enough to ask. He fills the silence with something else, something unsteady and bold. "What's left of you?"

For a moment, George silent. He examines the hand that's not slick and red, holding it to his side with uncertainty, like it might snap. Then he answers with a dull weight, like a package he isn't sure he should deliver: "My wits. Most of them, anyway." A wan smile cracks the seriousness of his face, and he reaches out, the smooth timber of his voice contrasting with the rough sounds of the old house. "Let's see what you made of me, Étienne."

Étienne's small, wiry fingers slip into the grown man's soft palm. It's hot and limp, but it holds, closing around Étienne's with a weak tremble.

He remembers its New Orleans-bound force.

The stories of George and his cleverness, his daring missions, his elaborate schemes. His movements, gestures, and words still show traces of those things.

But it's weak. Frail. Like the rest of him.

One angry old woman ran over the very best parts left trailing behind. The ropes connecting boy and woman exceed his strength. Not strong enough to hold his ground or make it past the battered armchair where he collapsed when he thought he still had the upper hand. Étienne pulls him closer, forcing the same careful calm into his voice. "You won't get out like the others," he says, and he's not sure if it's a warning or a promise. Maybe George isn't either.

Mr. Robichaux looks past him, toward the door that swallowed his oldest friend. They hear the creak of a floorboard. Muttering, humming, rocking—a fractured melody, back and forth. It stops there. It stays in the room. "No," he says, watching moving a furrowed brow. His eyes narrow. His breath steadies. "Not like the others."

The faint, familiar sounds fall back and disappear as quickly as they came. George straightens, faking more strength than he's found. They both pretend to believe it as he guides them toward the sofa, Étienne at his side. The storm still rages outside. Gusts of wind and lashing rain rattle through the creole cottage, battering it the way they battered George when his careless tongue and his reckless pride landed him in Big Mama's way. The sky is furious. Maybe angrier than her, but Étienne doubts it. Even when her sounds died and she slipped through the crack in his words, she was fiercer than anything he'd ever known. Surpassing storms, yet more wondrous. He tries to stop thinking about it. That fleeting moment holding her: the sensation. His eyes find George's again. They're softer now. Darker and sadder and more hopeful. Étienne sits, and George limps toward the map, beginning his strange, patchy story. "The trick," he says, looking over his shoulder at the boy, "is to know when you're beat. Before they do." His hand stretches toward a yellow pin, a series of thin lines, a crumpled chart that covers one unbroken wall of the living area. The aged house encircles it, a specter revisiting its former shell.

"Then why are you still here?" Étienne asks, thinking of all the other times George's pack and George's nerve were quicker than the boy who packed them. "Mémé's still dangerous. Even more now. And you're hurt."

Mr. Robichaux lets out a low chuckle, tired but smooth, as if he never intended for anyone else to hear it. "Why are you still here?" he says, the smile spreading to his eyes. The soft creases in his cheeks fill out as he raises his eyebrows, the tired man in front of Étienne younger and less beat than he seemed. The map points to something neither of them knows yet, but George is learning. George is watching.

The thunder rumbles and crashes, one loud roll into the next. George pulls the tattered sleeve of his shirt above the bandage, soaking up a few new drops of blood. He tries to hide the streaks of dark red, streaks of shame. "There's a lot you don't know, Étienne," he says, voice half velvet, half dirt. "A lot. I'm just beginning to understand myself." His hand gestures along the torn edge of the map, toward New Orleans and the bright spot where they've planted themselves. Where George Bruckner had to be dragged kicking and bleeding and powerless by the boy who shares his dark secrets. The Bruckner boy. "We have one job," George continues, his steps steadying. His fingers trace their path along the paper, away from Big Mama's last known location. Away from New Orleans and Louisiana and anywhere else that gave them trouble. Safe from workplace hazards. "One. And the old woman still got us. She got us good."

George shrugs his thin shoulders, loose but deliberate, like Étienne remembers her doing just a few minutes ago. "So, we have to try harder," he says, letting the words spill out and cross the room like they mean it. "This time we'll get it right." Étienne absorbs the words and the minor victory they wrap themselves in. The thin air grows thicker with the unsteady promise of them, but Étienne's unsteady too. He knows that kind of promise, and he knows George, his coward's heart. Observe the growing distance; the woman's fierceness intensifies, pain increases.

"It's bad," George goes on, not waiting for the boy to

challenge him. To update him: Still nothing. This time, someone sabotaged it. Neither minor setback nor slight problem, but a serious issue. Something deliberate. "Everywhere." The paper in front of him looks fragile and thin, each line carrying the weight of the words that should fill them, all of them heavier than they used to be. "Providence," George says, gesturing across the country. "Albany. Bangor. Poughkeepsie. Not as bad as here, not yet. But it will be. Our lot never quite seem to learn their lesson." Another sharp, low laugh. Less tired, less raw. "Like us." He turns back to Étienne, back to where they're both standing now. Back to New Orleans and everything Étienne ever knew. "She's been quiet for years, and we all forgot what the old devil was made of. What we were all made of. It almost cost us."

The boy nods, a quick and thoughtful bob of his curly head. He says nothing, doesn't have to. The pack. The nerve. They might be too quick for the rest of them, but George knows they're not quick enough for the little shadow of a brother who's learned his tricks. He softens his voice and settles into it, convincing himself as much as he convinces Étienne. "But here we are," he says, sinking into a chair. The green fabric, aged and stained, shows wear beyond its years. "Here we are," he repeats, fixing his eyes on the thin figure in front of him, fixing his loose grip on Étienne's sharp gaze. "We're too close now." It's not defeat. It's not. Not this time. It's something worse. Something less familiar, less clear. It starts with "d" George thinks, and it lingers longer than any bruise or any break: *determination*.

The sound of the storm rattles through the empty spaces, echoing the awful moment Étienne's command struck them both. They take the silence that follows, fill it with unfamiliar noises: the muffled howl of wind, the gentle brush of one bandaged hand across the map and the burning light it sends through the injured veins. The house emitted a frail voice. She stops there; Étienne remains. George wraps the piano scarf tighter. Not as tight as he could. Not as tight as Étienne will.

CHAPTER 11

THE PRICE OF POWER

É tienne's heart pounds. The storm assails the house like a vengeful spirit, spitting out rain and lightning with relentless persistence. He can almost taste the electricity as it fills the air, his mind buzzing with a name—Abaddon—that hum like a stubborn mosquito, impossible to ignore. Alone in the New Orleans home, he stands between the riotous wind and the hushed shadows, every nerve in his body taut. Lightning slashes through the darkness, revealing his tension-filled features and the tremor in his small posture. Each flash and roar seem to pulse with an unnatural fury, echoing the supernatural chaos that coils through the rooms and snakes inside him. Étienne shivers but remains still, mesmerized by the power crackling at the edges of his fear.

The storm escalates its assault on the house, thunder and lightning conspiring to rattle him. He senses something immense, something alive and aware of him. The word "Abaddon" drums in his head; its insistence sends a rush through his limbs that approaches a thrill. Is it a name? A warning? He stares upward, corners of the room, anticipating a call. His fingers twitch, and he clenches them into fists, unsure whether to fight or embrace this sensation. Another rumble of thunder shakes the floorboards; the storm seems to fill every space.

The echo of "Abaddon" grows louder and more insistent; Étienne presses his hands against his ears in vain. The name thrums through him, threading his veins with an electric current that vibrates with an eerie potential. Closing his eyes, he hears only one sound—a whisper merging with a roar. The floor makes noise as his weight changes, and he tries to stay motionless. Curiosity pulls at his fear, urging him to stay and understand this terrifying thing that is also his.

Étienne takes a breath, opening his eyes to the room washed in ghostly light. He wonders if the storm outside hears the same word he does, if it's raging because it knows he's inside, knows he's watching. Rain pummels the windowpanes. His stomach rejects the possibility—is it true? He flinches as lightning cuts the sky in jagged lines, leaving afterimages that dance like specters before him. The sensation buzzing inside him is like an echo of the storm, a force of nature awakening with relentless momentum.

Turning from the windows, Étienne's eyes find the shadows creeping across the walls. They seem alive, part of the same supernatural force that's invaded the house and his mind. His mouth goes dry, and he swallows hard, wondering if he's only imagining their shift and stretch toward him. A chill runs down his spine; his heart thrums with the rhythm of a thousand whispers, all speaking the same name. His fear sits heavy, but underneath it, a new emotion stirs—a fierce, unsettling hunger for whatever power those shadows might hold.

The wind shrieks around the house; "Abaddon" crashes over him like waves on a storm-battered shore. He tries to focus on it, but it's like holding onto smoke. Étienne clutches at his arms; tension fills his muscles as if they belong to someone else. The sensation becomes tangible—a wire pulled tight inside him—and he wonders how long it can hold before snapping. A larger part of him desires to witness the outcome.

With a slow, hesitant step, Étienne inches closer to the center of the room. The space has a charged atmosphere, as if it's waiting for him to claim it. Darkness descends. His stance was a testament to his courage, a defiant stand against fear. Unlike Buddy, he is the sole recipient of the rewards this time. Amidst the storm's loud howl, he clenches his teeth to show his power despite his fear. His pulse throbs in his throat, matching the madness outside.

Rain continues to hammer the windows; Étienne knows it would be easy to run, to hide under covers or lock himself in the safety of his room. But this time he stays, letting the furious storm match his own rising tempest, knowing the supernatural conflict will find him wherever he goes. He senses a looming decision, as charged as the lightning cracking overhead. His lips part, breathless with the effort of standing firm.

"Abaddon" flares once more, then dies into a searing silence. Étienne gasps—almost surprised to hear himself—and experiences the edges of the room, blurring with the impossible roar of the storm as it reaches its ominous crescendo.

CHAPTER 12

RENÉE'S RETURN

The front door moans on its hinges as Renée and T-Bone step into the murky living room, bringing with them the drum of rain on the roof. Renée's eyes comb the shadows with determined exhaustion. T-Bone surveys his surroundings. He sees everything that's amiss. He notes the dented table, the disorder, a careless soul in every object. Étienne is near the doorway, as nervous as a stray cat. His fingers fumble with a scrap of cloth. He tries to hide it in the dark, where Renée can't see. His hand shakes when T-Bone leans toward him, murmurs something low and warning. Renée's stare makes her suspicions clear. Her son is in trouble again.

"Everything okay?" T-Bone sets his jaw as he asks this, more pointedly now.

Étienne shrugs. His reply is a low, mumbled murmur audible over the rain. "Said I'm fine."

He spoke in a shaky, protective tone, his hands trembling. Renée joins him, her gaze fixed upon the hidden cloth. She kneels to lift his chin.

"This?" She holds the torn piece of shirt. Her voice is gentle but urgent. "The chair? What's happened, bébé?"

Étienne struggles to hold her gaze. Opening his mouth, he

closes it and hesitates. With hunched shoulders, he averts his gaze, struggling to find an answer. He exclaimed, "I handled it. Handled it on my own."

Renée's eyes widen. T-Bone cuts in, louder now, demanding. "Don't lie. What did you promise me?"

Étienne goes pale. He stammers, fearful, and the words tumble out. "I didn't mean to do it. I didn't! They started it."

T-Bone and Renée exchanged glances. She gets to her feet, touching her son's arm. "Who?" she asks. "Who's they?"

Étienne fumbles for words, his breathing unsteady. He doesn't know, he says, voice still shaky. Renée's questions come rapid-fire, more intense, each word pushing against Étienne's resolve.

"Is it them?" she demands. "From Providence? The ones who broke into the house?"

Étienne hesitates, and she presses him again.

"Amalie's dream? Is that what she saw?"

"Non!" Étienne blurts. "No. It's not the same."

Her eyes bore into his. "Did they hurt you?"

"They didn't do anything!"

"Are you sure?" Her voice softens a little, and she cups his chin in her hand. "Are you?"

Étienne's eyes dart between them. His hand still trembles as he clutches his torn shirt, but his tone grows bolder, defiant. "No one's here now," he insists. "Just me. I scared them away."

Renée looks relieved and worried. Her eyes are wide with disbelief. She urges him again, softer this time, to tell the truth.

"Isn't lying," Étienne mumbles. "Told you already. I handled it."

T-Bone makes a frustrated noise and crosses his arms. "Like in Providence, huh?" His voice is rough with skepticism. "And that worked out how?"

Étienne presses his lips together. There's anger in the way he clenches his fists. "Maybe things are different now."

Renée's voice cuts through, authoritative and sharp. "Étienne."

His name hangs in the air like an accusation. He glares at the floor, teeth set against a dozen replies.

T-Bone eases, arguing with a sigh. "I'll stay close," he says, more softly, more brotherly. "I'll be around, okay?"

There's relief and something resentful in Étienne's voice. "That what you did today?"

T-Bone holds his gaze. "Things are different," he echoes. "Told you they would be."

Renée squeezes Étienne's shoulder with gentle insistence. "Come straight to me, bébé. When things happen, don't hide them."

She smiles when she says he scared her half to death. Relief shows on her face, yet her smile weakens. She surveys the room, noting the overturned chairs are not the only problem. Inscrutable shadows baffle her.

The tension loosens its grip on the small house as Renée, T-Bone, Étienne, and Amalie gather in the living room. They move like tired ghosts among the clutter, like bodies floating in water. Lamplight leaves faint shadows on faded Creole furniture. T-Bone sinks into a battered armchair. He speaks in a measured tone, recalls a piece of their past. Despite his bruised shoulder, his voice remains steady. Renée interjects, combining the memory with practicality. Amalie clutches her doll and listens, wide-eyed.

Étienne avoids mention of the chaos. He nods as the others talk. The nostalgic memory brought a comforting warmth. The ensuing silence reignites the tension, reminding them of the lingering danger in their home.

"It's good being here again," T-Bone says. There's a note of relief. "Almost forgot how it felt, being settled."

Renée gives a dry laugh. "Settled," she echoes, looking at the jumble of books on the floor.

Amalie perks up at the sound of her mother's voice. T-Bone ruffles her hair and winks. "You don't even remember, do you, Dolly? Not like this one." He gestures to Étienne.

"Do too," Amalie pipes. She surprises him. "Whitford Street. Had the white door and stairs up to the porch. You made the truck with the marker, remember? And Mémé's room smelled funny. There was music on the walls."

"From next door," Renée explains. "She loved the old phonograph."

"And nightmares," Amalie whispers.

Renée's expression shifts from surprise to concern. She squeezes Amalie's shoulder. "Oh, chérie, they're nothing to be scared of. Moving's hard, but this was safest for everyone."

Étienne stares into the lamplight, silent and tight-lipped. Amalie glances at him, then buries her face against Renée's arm. T-Bone frowns and breaks the mood.

"Lot of jazz here," he says with a grin, shifting the conversation. "Even the radio. Think that'll get boring?"

Renée makes an amused sound. "Better than Elvis on the jukebox?"

"The diner!" T-Bone chuckles, taking her cue. "We always stopped by."

He's pleased when Amalie giggles. Étienne grows a little more relaxed. "Whole place knew us," T-Bone continues. "That old man and his big cheeseburgers."

"You loved those burgers," Renée teases. "Always hungry back there."

Étienne sinks into the couch, watching them. There's the hint of a smile as Renée recalls birthday dinners at the diner.

"Remember one where you brought the entire class?" She eyes Étienne. Her eyes hold questions, hopeful and probing. "Making new friends yet?"

He shrugs. His expression clouds, and he evades her questions with vague, mumbled answers.

"Just give it time," she encourages, but he doesn't respond.

Étienne leans forward, pretends to be interested in the ragged book by his feet. T-Bone rubs his sore shoulder. Renée sits with Amalie, her fatigue etched in the deep lines of her face. She brushes a curl of hair from the child's forehead.

"Dolly's going to sleep soon," she says. "Wants the rest of her story first, I bet."

T-Bone smiles. "Better make me one too. One that looks like me."

"Wouldn't like it," Amalie mumbles. "Not if it came to life."

Renée and T-Bone exchange a glance. She asks if they're moving again and if that's why she heard them talking about Providence. She's more than a whisper now, her eyes wide, brimming with tears. "Tienne's mean to me."

"Was not," Étienne protests, going red. "I didn't even—"

"You were," Amalie insists, turning to Renée. She pleads for an explanation.

Renée holds Amalie close and rocks her back and forth. "You know why," she says, weary but tender. "You do."

Her voice fills with false certainty. "New Orleans is home, bébé. Not going anywhere."

Amalie clutches her doll tighter. Renée gives T-Bone a worried expression. He leans forward to catch Amalie's eye, talking like he's telling a ghost tale.

"The girl went all the way to town for her thread," he begins. "It was dark, and the wind was howling."

Amalie wipes her eyes and pays attention. She loves hearing stories from T-Bone.

"Then what happened?" she prompts, but her voice trembles. "What if she didn't?"

"Didn't what?"

"Make it back."

Renée takes a deep breath. "She did," she assures, smiling. "She made it back with the finest spool you ever saw."

"She didn't need to run away to finish her doll." T-Bone looks at Amalie, his expression serious but soft. "Was already alive."

Even Étienne is listening now, half stewing over the accusation, half focused on his brother's tale. When T-Bone reaches the end, everyone but Étienne is smiling. Renée gives Amalie a last hug.

"Say goodnight to Mémé before bed," she tells her.

"Can't," Amalie argues. "Not without Lucille." Her expression remains fixed.

Renée gives her a gentle nudge. "Better find her, then," she says with a wink.

Amalie runs off to search for the doll. Silence settles like a draft under the door. Étienne stares hard at the floor. He breaks the silence with sudden force, his voice filled with uncertainty.

"So we're staying?"

Renée looks surprised. "Told you," she answers. "That's what we're doing."

"Even if weird things happen?"

Her reply is firm, though she's shaken. "We're staying."

He's not convinced. "Even if it gets worse?"

"Don't say that," Renée insists. "Not again."

"But what if—"

"It doesn't matter," she interrupts, cutting him off. She wants him to believe this. "We're all together. That's enough."

T-Bone nods in agreement, but his voice is strained. "We'll figure it out. Together, like she said."

"Like before," Étienne snaps. His voice dripped with disdain, each syllable a venomous barb.

Renée is silent. She looks weary, like she can't manage another word.

"Could we? T-Bone?"

T-Bone winces as he stands. "Sure thing, Dolly. I'll check on you and Lucille." He pauses in the doorway. He looks back at Étienne, hesitates, then leaves them alone.

Renée watches the floorboards with caution, like they're fragile. She turns down the light, perches on the arm of the couch.

"Listen to me, bébé," she says. "Just listen."

Her presence is gentle and comforting, but the strain is clear. "Not easy for any of us," she admits, a sigh in her voice. "I know."

Étienne avoids her gaze. "They're coming again, aren't they?"

"Don't," she begs. "Please."

He turns away, unwilling to give in.

"Be a long night," she tells him. "Want to be up for it?"

The question lingers. He doesn't answer.

"Had long nights before, you and me." She's weary but intent. "Remember?"

Étienne doesn't respond. She keeps trying.

"Rain, so much rain, and we couldn't sleep, so we stayed up with you and let you laugh." Her hand rests on his hair, her voice catching. "We'll figure it out, like he said. We always have."

Étienne sits in silence.

"We will this time, too. I promise." Her words linger in the dark as she leaves him there, alone in the dim room.

CHAPTER 13

THE SENILE SEER

Étienne stands by the silent phone, alone in the dim living room. The hum of the city outside weaves through the open windows like a hot, sticky thread. He runs a finger over the faded wallpaper, wondering if he should call his older brother about Mémé and her unsettling words. But then he'd know Étienne's fear, that he lacks the bravery others presume. He paces, glancing up at his brother's photo on the mantel, hoping for an answer. The wooden floor creaks and settles under his restless feet.

He picks up the phone again, then puts it back down. Sweat glistens on his hand from where it grips the plastic receiver. What if his brother just laughs? Étienne can almost hear his voice, teasing him from miles away. "Scared of a little old lady? That's funny, Ti-Jean." That idea makes him wince. But then another thought pushes in, one that pulls at him hard. What if his brother believes him? What if he understands? He could even return. Étienne imagines his steady footsteps filling the quiet house, his voice pushing back all the things Étienne can't handle alone. He picks up the phone again, heart tripping over itself. But no. What if he tells him, and his brother doesn't care? What if he feels he's weak and doesn't bother with him at all?

His eyes flick to T-Bone's picture. The photograph on the mantel makes his brother look strong and sure, not a single ounce of doubt in his wide smile. It's from a few months back, right before they moved here. Right before everything got strange.

He paces, avoiding the photo's gaze. T-Bone's expertise would resolve this. T-Bone never doubted himself like Étienne does. His brother wouldn't fear the old lady and her stories. Even if Mémé was strange, T-Bone wouldn't care. The chill from her words about his future still affects Étienne. Her voice echoes in his head, certain and soft. She called him to her room, speaking of power, blood, and gifts. It's his turn now, and he must not disappoint.

Étienne circles back to the mantel, hesitating again at the phone. He doesn't want to bother T-Bone. Out in the wide, exhilarating world, his brother is attending school and building new relationships. Living the life, Étienne wishes he had. He's already so busy, already so far away. But then Étienne's stomach twists as he remembers Mémé's words. As he senses the shadows from her room creeping back in. What if he's not strong enough to deal with it alone? What if he needs his brother more than he's letting himself admit? That idea diminishes him, as if he's contracting into the recesses of the large, vacant residence.

He reaches for the phone, the room silent except for the sound of his shallow breaths. But then he snatches his hand back, eyes darting to the photo. His face tightens, determination mingled with fear. Once more, he reaches for his phone. T-Bone is someone he doesn't want to need. His aspiration is to be strong. Staring at the picture, he struggles to decide.

Étienne stands by the silent phone, fingers clenched around the receiver. Fear and indecision war within him. The house settles around him, dark and muted. His own breath is the only sound. A figure appears at the edge of the hallway, making him jump.

He drops the phone. Mr. Robichaux gives a cautious smile, like he understands Étienne's turmoil. The floorboards sigh under his heavy steps as he walks over and presses something into Étienne's hand—a carved wooden charm.

"Keep this close," Mr. Robichaux's voice is low.

Étienne desires to accept his words, but questions if a piece of wood can shield him from the unusual things within his family.

The charm is small and rough in some places, smooth in others. Étienne stares at it, turning it over in his hand. The designs carved into the wood are more like scratches than symbols—nothing familiar. Mr. Robichaux stands there, waiting for Étienne to say something, his eyes bright.

"Why?" Étienne glances between Mr. Robichaux and the charm. "What is it?" His voice comes out thin.

Mr. Robichaux keeps smiling, but there's a seriousness behind it now—someone who's had practice keeping secrets. His hand rests on Étienne's shoulder, heavy but careful.

"Just keep it with you, Ti-Jean," he says. "It'll help more than you think."

Étienne frowns—the wood is flimsy in his palm—how can this little thing protect him?

He recalled Mémé's words; they eclipsed everything, leaving only her voice and the gravity of her message. She was so sure. So clear. Étienne grips the charm tighter, searching Mr. Robichaux's face for something to hold on to.

"How do you know?" Étienne tries not to sound scared.

Mr. Robichaux's smile softens. "Let's just say I've seen a thing or two," he replies, not giving away much. Although his voice was soothing, Étienne's doubts lingered.

Étienne glances down at the charm again. He wants it to be enough. He wants to trust Mr. Robichaux and the strange knowledge he seems to carry. Mémé's strength was undeniable, a force he couldn't ignore. Though elderly and feeble in appearance, she gives off a creepy vibe, as if she's watching him from all angles, even when her gaze meets his.

Étienne shudders, remembering her sightless gaze—the words she'd spoken still stick to him, making him itch with fear. Mr. Robichaux's hand squeezes his shoulder as if sensing Étienne's hesitation.

"Mémé can't touch you when you have this." Mr. Robichaux gestures to the charm, speaking to ensure Étienne catches every word. "You'll be safe."

Étienne remembers Mr. Robichaux fixing the gate, a pointed gaze hinting at something more. Étienne witnessed Mr. Robichaux's incense burning and salt sprinkling rituals; he always handled strange occurrences. Étienne wants to ask how much he knows about Mémé—about all the dark, spooky stuff that's been closing in on them since they got here. But he just nods, uncertain of the truth.

Mr. Robichaux nods back as if they're agreeing on something bigger than both of them. He pulls his hand away and vanishes around the corner, leaving Étienne standing there with the charm and a mess of tangled thoughts. The house is silent again—no footsteps, no voices—just Étienne and the nervous flutter in his chest. He rubs his thumb over the carved wood, experiencing the strange marks press into his skin. He tries to picture the charm doing what Mr. Robichaux says it will—he tries to imagine the awful chill of Mémé's presence being blocked by a tiny piece of wood.

Étienne doesn't know if it's possible—he doesn't know what to do with the scraps of hope the charm leaves him—but he clings to it anyway, stuffing the charm deep into his pocket. He glances at his phone, considering a quick check with T-Bone.

◆ ◆ ◆

Étienne glances between the phone and the hallway, uncertainty gnawing at him. The charm in his pocket presses into his leg. Before he can reach for the phone again, a new presence appears. He startles, remembering Mémé and all her terrible promises. But it's only Ms. Devereaux, standing in the doorway with one eyebrow raised as if she's caught him at something.

"Everything all right, Étienne?" Her tone implies prior knowledge of its falsehood.

"It's fine." His voice cracks.

"Just fine?" The words hang between them as Étienne looks at the floor.

Ms. Devereaux scrutinizes him. "And how's your family, Étienne? Your grandma settling in all right?" He flinches, surprised by how much she knows. "I hear you've had some strange happenings around here." Her voice drops to a near whisper. "I wouldn't be surprised if things start to get a little spooky. Not with a family like yours." Étienne's stomach tightens.

"I see it all the time," Ms. Devereaux continues. "People like you get a little lost when the dark forces are close." Her words make Étienne's skin prickle, even more than the charm does. "You're in a special place, Étienne. These old houses, these old streets—they've seen a lot." She takes a step closer. "I think you can handle it."

Étienne's not so sure. What's the source of her extensive knowledge concerning them? About him? He is dizzy with the possibilities.

"I don't know what you mean," he says, but he isn't fooling anyone.

Ms. Devereaux laughs as if she finds his attempt to act endearing. "Oh, I think you do," she says. "It helps to have someone who understands. Who knows what it's like?"

Ms. Devereaux nods, as if she understands his thoughts. Her

smile doesn't fade as she turns to leave. "Think about it, Étienne."

Étienne stands there, alone with his thoughts. He touches the charm in his pocket, its edges poking into his skin. Ms. Devereaux's confidence regarding the strange occurrences was striking. Her words eased his isolation, but not enough to end his concerns. Not enough to stop wondering what Mémé is planning for him, or what the awful powers he's inherited will mean. Maybe she's right. Maybe he can handle it. But right now, all he wants is to call T-Bone and receive confirmation from his brother that none of it's real.

CHAPTER 14

EMBRACING THE LEGACY

Étienne begins his exploration in the cramped hallway of the Laurent home. His small fingers trail along the dusty wood paneling, searching for any hint of Mémé's hidden occult books. He notices a faded wall. A loose floorboard uncovers a secret compartment. Inside are old, leather-bound letters and a small, tarnished key. He flips it open, and his breath catches. The light from a single lamp casts long shadows across the floors, and each step echoes his determination and apprehension. His hands quiver as he picks up a scrap of paper inscribed with strange symbols. His heart pounds in time with the storm brewing outside, reinforcing his resolve to follow in Mémé's footsteps.

The letters are heavy and brittle in his hands, ink smeared and fading. He turns one over, trying to decipher the spidery writing that crawls across the paper. A strange excitement knots with fear in his stomach. Étienne listens to the silence of the house, waiting for any sound that might mean he'll have to shove everything back where it came from and pretend he's asleep in bed. But it's only the old floors settling and the distant hum of music, and he sinks down to the ground, flipping open the topmost letter.

Time is slippery. He thinks about the word, "Hastur," an

accidental meeting of his eyes with paper as he gathers the old letters into his lap. He moves his lips over the name, remembering half-heard stories, the uneasiness that settles over grownups when they think he's not listening.

His fingers brush against the key, smooth and cold, and he lifts it up, dangling it in front of his face. Its diminutive size allowed him to wear it as a neck charm. "Some day," he thinks, "everyone's gonna see how brave I really am." He closes his hand around the key, letting it press into his palm as he lifts another of the letters, studying the indecipherable scrawl.

A thump from a nearby room makes him pause. Waiting, he holds his breath, but the sound doesn't return. He's alone, the house creaking with the storm's arrival. Scrambling to gather his discoveries, he exhales, shoves the key into his pocket, and stuffs everything back into the hidden space. He leaves them there, in case the sound comes back.

Étienne's curiosity pulls him deeper into the shadowy house. He reaches for a door with peeling paint, fingers hesitant on the handle. It sticks, and for a moment, he thinks it won't open. But then it flies wide with a creak that makes him flinch.

He stops in the threshold, looking into the shadowy space beyond. A table sits in the center, with a bare bulb swaying above it. He's never dared to enter this part of the house before. But Mémé's been silent, too silent, and Étienne suspects she's waiting for something.

Étienne waits, too, still as a mouse as he decides whether to risk it. He steps twice; a gust of stale air from the closing door propels him inside.

Magazines and news clippings stack high on the table. Drawings and notes lie tangled together. The urge to touch and understand is like a pulse in his fingertips.

He walks toward the table, steps lighter now as he gains confidence. A sudden rush of energy makes him powerful and big.

He reaches out to the nearest pile, catching sight of a photograph half-buried beneath a yellowed map of the French Quarter. The photo is small, an old-fashioned print with white borders. Five people stand in a group, stiff and serious, with shadows all around them.

Another noise comes from the hallway, this time a high, whining sound. Étienne holds still, not breathing, certain he'll see Mémé's ghost if he turns around.

The energy of discovery courses through him, and Étienne experiences a kind of reckless courage. That kid is more than just scared. He's the one with the knowledge now.

He picks up the journal, its pages thin. "No use," he thinks. "I can't do this with everything hidden." He stuffs it into his shirt.

Étienne's hands darted over the uncovered treasure in the safety of his own cramped room. He fills in the details, scrawling answers over the parts that make little sense. He pins the completed pages to his walls.

The scraps and letters spill out from the bottom of his closet, and Étienne leans against the door, watching them. Swinging from his fingers, the old key, its tarnished surface catching the lamplight, is in his hand. The storm builds around the house, but his breathing is steady, his lips moving over the word he found: Hastur.

Étienne's search leads him into the dim, cluttered study where Ms. Devereaux waits among shelves of ancient volumes and dormant paraphernalia. She greets him with a soft, measured tone. "I taught in Providence," she remarks, sliding a rusted metal box across a creaking oak desk toward him. Her gaze flicks over the scattered artifacts while Étienne listens, his eyes widening with both nervous excitement and latent recognition of powers stirring within him. The room vibrates with the sound of distant thunder and the steady drip of rain against cracked windowpanes. As Ms. Devereaux explains clues from the artifacts in clear, concise dialogue, Étienne's hand brushes against the cool metal of the mysterious key he found, linking the two revelations in a single, profound moment of discovery.

Wind slams the door; Étienne pauses, observing the room and his instructor. He didn't expect her to be waiting for him, but it shouldn't be a surprise. Ms. Devereaux has always been a step ahead of him, stirring something between curiosity and distrust inside him. He can't read her like he can other adults, and it puts him on edge.

"Étienne," she breaks the silence, "I've been expecting you. I trust you found what you were looking for?" She nods to his shirt where the journal's ragged edges stick out of the waistband. His hand goes to cover it, but he catches himself in time and lets it drop to his side. "I don't know," he admits. "Maybe." His voice sounds unsure, even to him. "Mémé never said what all this stuff was for."

Ms. Devereaux stands, pushing her chair back from the desk with a creak. "Your grandmother's intentions are obvious, but I know she's preparing you for something significant." She moves to a shelf crowded with books and other strange objects, running a finger along their spines before turning back to him. "Significant," she repeats. "And dangerous, if you don't understand it."

Étienne's shoulders stiffen, and he glances at the door, feeling the weight of the house outside it. But then she slides the rusted box toward him, and the motion pulls him back. "Your mother was very bright," she says, "but she chose a different path." Her eyes catch his again, more serious this time. "What kind of path do you intend to choose?"

He stares at the box, words like the ones he saw in the hallway floating through his head, refusing to settle into anything he can use. The box seems to be locked, but the clasp swings loose under his touch. He opens it, sees yellowed papers and bits of strange-looking equipment. There's a piece of jewelry on top, something like a thin bracelet or a child's ring, and he pulls it out. "I don't even know where to start," he admits.

Ms. Devereaux picks up the bracelet, studying the odd symbols that circle it before setting it back inside the box. "Understanding is the first step," she tells him. "Understanding and making sure others do not misunderstand." She nods to the chaotic room around them. "You see why I brought you here?"

Étienne nods, but he doesn't understand. Not really. "I'm the youngest," he blurts out without meaning to. He disdains incomprehension; still, it remains. He spoke in a muted voice, almost a whisper. "What if I mess it up?"

"You will," she replies, and his eyes go wide. His blood ran cold at her confession, the unspoken fear he'd harbored voiced. "But that's part of learning. You have to make mistakes if you're going to succeed."

Étienne swallows. "Mémé never said that."

Ms. Devereaux gives him a thin, knowing smile. "I suspect she never did."

Thunder vibrates the room, rain a steady rhythm against the windowpanes. Étienne's eyes narrow on the ornate mirror as it rattles on the shelf, and he moves toward it, curious. A blurred reflection, less face, more ink stain, shimmers on the silver. He blinks and rubs his eyes, thinking he's too tired to see straight.

"It's best not to stare at that for too long," Ms. Devereaux warns, lifting the mirror from the shelf and setting it down on the desk beside him. Étienne recoils, sending papers flying.

Ms. Devereaux watches as he crams the letters into his pockets. Instead of helping, she picks up a photograph and turns it over in her hands. He waits, but she remains silent. It makes him want it even more, and she holds it out to him.

"This was taken in the room you found last night," she says above the storm. He looks at the picture, focusing on his mother's stern face. "It used to be your family's favorite gathering place," Ms. Devereaux continues, "until certain connections became too risky."

Étienne says nothing, just stares at the photo. Feeling her eyes on him, he reflects on fleeing from the secret room last night, standing in the hallway with a racing heart and fists clenched. His imagination inventing every horrible scenario as he waited for the ghostly noise to come again. It didn't, and this morning, upon waking, he was braver, bolder. Ready to take on anything.

But now he's not so sure. The weight of the old house settles over him, and he clutches the photograph, uncertain. His voice shakes just a little when he speaks. "You think it's safe, then?"

"For some," she says, "if they're prepared. But it's not for me to say whether you're among them."

The room grows silent, except for the drip of water from the leaky window frame. He fidgets, nervous, but Ms. Devereaux says nothing more. She watches him with that strange, knowing look and he stands, rubbing his damp palms on his shirt.

"I've got more of Mémé's things at home," he tells her, holding the photograph close against his chest. "I don't know what most of it means."

"That's why you came here," Ms. Devereaux replies. "To find out." Her words echo off the bare walls and Étienne hears the finality in them. She means for him to leave and his heart races as he gathers the objects, the letters, the scraps of knowledge.

He crosses the room, stopping when he reaches the door. He refused to yield, facing her again. "Were you Mémé's teacher?" he asks.

She sidesteps the question. "I taught in Providence," she repeats. "Your grandmother spent some time there."

The name sends a chill down Étienne's spine, but the pieces are already fitting together in his mind. He might understand more than she wishes.

"Okay," he says, opening the door and stepping out into the dark hallway, less afraid than before.

The rain lets up as he makes his way home. The house is silent when he enters, everyone busy with their own business or out running errands. He's glad for the silence. It gives him time to spread his new discoveries over the kitchen table.

The nervous energy builds in him as he draws the shades against the dying light, pins maps and charts to the wall, lays Mémé's old letters out in patterns only he can see. They form shapes that twist and loop, symbols that come together as he links the two revelations.

The key is heavy in his hand as he turns it over and over, and a slight smile pulls at his lips. He knows where it fits. He knows what to do. With the knowledge, plans, and the house to himself, the storm's sounds have faded, replaced by his breathing and the unsteady beat of his heart.

CHAPTER 15

MÉMÉ'S DARK INHERITANCE

Étienne stands in the doorway, listening to Mémé's rhythmic snores. His stomach twists with nerves. He pictured this room, a maze; hours of searching yielding nothing. Now that he is here, it feels much smaller. He might escape unnoticed if he's quick. A streak of lightning flares outside, throwing warped shadows through the boards on the windows. He must find those books.

He creeps in and holds his breath. Faded curtains obscure the windows, obscuring the time. Incense burns low in the corner, hiding, smelling dust and rot. Étienne pokes around shelves filled with old figurines and jumbled messes. Something lurks here. He senses it, and he must locate it before anyone sees him searching. Shuffling, he kicks up motes of dust that make him cough and sneeze. He goes to the corner where smelling incense blends with cigarette smoke and stale perfume. Big Mama's chair looms above him, her reading glasses dangling from its side. It makes him shiver.

Étienne turns away and focuses on the rows of books on the opposite wall. These aren't what he seeks, commonplace novels and educational items. He runs his fingers over them, anyway, hoping one might tip forward and reveal a hidden passage.

Nothing. Étienne wants to scream, but he grits his teeth and moves to a low chest. 1800s-style baby clothes fill it. He wants to dump them out and kick them across the room. He clutches his fists. Mémé's low snore pierces the silence, reminding him how close he is to getting caught.

He crouches beside the bed and pulls up the long quilt that drags on the floor. Her blind eyes stare at the ceiling. Even in her sleep, Big Mama looks like she knows what he is up to. He imagines her sitting up and shouting, "What's that boy doing?" He backs away and turns to a large wooden cabinet. Inside, he finds boxes of thread and a dead bug. His hands tremble with frustration as he bangs the drawers shut. Why did they come here? He liked Providence. He liked their apartment. His friends were well-liked by him. He tries to swallow the thought, knowing it won't hone anything.

Étienne almost gave up before discovering a loose cabinet panel. His pulse quickens. He scrapes his knuckles, tugging at the rough wood, but it swings open to reveal a cramped space stuffed with faded paper and broken trinkets. The bottom holds a jumble of old coins and metal charms. Some of them appear familiar, like things he has seen street vendors sell to tourists. He holds a cold metal crucifix in his palm, remembering the day they moved into the house. Two women on the porch had crossed themselves when they passed by. One of them looked right at Étienne and said to the other, "That's where that family moved to."

Yellowed receipts and doctor's notes also fill the compartment. Étienne unfolds them, one by one. Words like "stillborn" and "infant death" jump out at him, making his stomach knot with guilt. His sister Margaret had whispered about it in Providence before they left. Étienne thought she was being mean to make him stop following her. Now, he isn't so sure. He shoves the papers into his pocket, experiencing sickness, excitement, and terror.

He reaches deeper and finds a small stack of photographs.

The faces in them appear like ghosts. unfamiliar faces appear: a slender man in overalls, plus two women who appear despondent. One has Big Mama's long hair. Étienne stares at it until he is sure, then flips through the rest. The house groans, settling. Sweat slicked his palms as his pulse pounded, a frantic rhythm against the innocent world inside him. He stared unblinking at the silhouette before him, incapable of looking away from the threatening figure that towered ahead.

The air thickened, charged with an electric current that sent tremors through his body. The acrid scent of fear filled his nostrils, sharpening his senses to a razor's edge. Dread and anticipation twisted in his gut, coiling tighter with each passing second. He stood frozen, his gaze fixed on the menacing silhouette that loomed ahead, a dark promise of what was to come.

One photo has names written on the back: Maggie, Francis, Charlie. Étienne wonders why no one told him. He wonders what else they aren't saying. He digs past the photographs, looking for more. The lights flicker, and a heavy gust rattles the windows. Mémé shifts in her bed, her snore catching in her throat. Étienne freezes.

A lull followed the storm, but a charged atmosphere remained. Étienne tucks the papers further into his pocket. He must learn what they mean, what all of this means. His legs feel weak as he stands, bracing himself against the cabinet. He fears getting caught. He fears what he'll find if he doesn't.

Étienne's hand trembles as he lifts the small, leather-bound book from the stack of papers. The embossed symbols on the cover seem to squirm beneath his fingers. His breath catches. He traces the shapes, his gaze captivated. His imagination runs wild with stories of cults and curses and things his mother says he is too young to hear. The air is thick with dust and anticipation as he opens the cover. Inscriptions appear inside; some are familiar, others his. How did they get here? Étienne whispers, "New Orleans... Providence..." and his breath comes faster as he reads the words again and again. His pulse is loud in his ears, thumping like footsteps coming to get him.

He flips back to the first page. More words. Long words. Unnatural words. They run together like spells. Étienne thinks of the photographs and papers he stuffed into his pocket, the names of family members he has never met. He imagines them finding this book, hiding it away, hoping that one day someone else would come along to take it. To take Big Mama's place.

Étienne turns the page again. One incantation stands out from the rest. He stares at it until the letters go fuzzy. He could have written this yesterday. The thought makes his skin prickle. His name's absence is insignificant. He slams the book shut and throws it into the pile of papers.

The wind intensifies, howling through the cracks in the windows. Étienne's curiosity battles with his fear, compelling his hand to reach for the book. He feels the urge to uncover its secrets. Picking it up once more, he flips through the pages quicker this time. The longer he gazes at the content, the more it starts to make sense. Everything he needs seems to be right there. Familiar words from his time in Providence are intertwined with unfamiliar ones. "New Orleans," he reads aloud. "Providence." Again. And again.

Mémé's secrets. His secrets.

He says it aloud. "Providence. New Orleans. How did they get here?" The wind answers with another mournful howl.

He remembers Big Mama telling the grownups about the old house. "This is where I was strongest," she said. "He'll find us again. Just wait." His parents hushed her and called it rambling. Étienne disagrees. He presses his finger into the embossed cover. The symbols blur, and he whispers, "He's found us already."

Étienne hugs the book to his chest and closes his eyes,

sensing the words from its pages pulse through him. They sting like a hundred red ants. How did they get here? "Providence," he says. "New Orleans."

The room goes darker as the storm clouds gather outside. Night approaches. They will notice he is missing. Étienne stuffs the book under his shirt, the cool leather pressing against his ribs. He closes the compartment and watches the door, expecting Mémé to appear any second. She knows he has been here. She knows what he has found.

Étienne backs toward the hallway. His pulse races with both fear and fascination. He can't take his eyes off the loose panel. The smell of incense and leather follows him, choking the air with secrets.

He clutches the book and runs, forgetting to breathe.

CHAPTER 16

THE NEW VESSEL RISES

The room appears small as Étienne thumbs through a thick book, letters too strange to most eyes spelling out words he grasps with difficulty. Although everyone else returned to New Orleans, he believes that this place remains haunted. Sunlight struggles through the kitchen window, like it's not welcome here, like it knows the house belongs to him. His sister's eyes are all nerves and little girl terror. Ignoring her, he pushes through, wanting to prove his bravery. He says the words out loud and tries not to stutter.

Étienne leans in close over the book, his finger gliding along each faded line. The room's too bright for what he's doing, but closing the window shades would make him seem weak. He tries not to notice the sun dancing across the table and stays fixed on the letters. The smell of gumbo and incense clings to the air, wrapping itself around him like it's testing his resolve. The table's uneven, one leg shorter than the rest, and it rocks a little every time he turns a page. He sets his jaw and pretends the wobble doesn't matter.

He can't keep pretending he's alone. His sister is right there, her chair almost too big for her tiny frame. Étienne glances in her direction. She doesn't flinch, not for one second. He knows she's scared, but she's got this strange way of staring like she's rooting for him, like she's waiting to see if her big brother will fail. She picks at a loose thread on her dress, her hair a messy cloud around her head. "Étienne?" she whispers. Her voice sounds as frail as she looks.

He ignores her and keeps going. He recalls parts of that thick, worn book from Providence. This is the first time he's read it since they came back to New Orleans. There's pressure behind his eyes and he wants it to go away. "Étienne?" Her voice has more nerve this time. It's an accusation and a question all rolled up in one. The house creaks, and Étienne wonders if it's answering her.

The book is the most important thing. Despite Amalie's presence, her poking and prodding left him as a scared child. He needs to finish it, needs to push through. Failure means remaining a boy who fears shadows. The letters swirl in front of him, and he takes a deep breath, waiting for the shapes to settle. He thinks about what it would be like to master all of it, to show Buddy he's not the runt anymore. He notices the way Amalie looks at him. It's like he's breaking a toy she loves.

His mouth is dry, and the words are strange. They twist and bend and pull at him like they know he's not ready. "You'll see," he mutters, more to himself than to her. The letters seem to smirk, like they've got his number. Étienne stayed focused, despite Amalie curling up. She doesn't understand his sense of smallness. He pushes out a breath and says the next line.

He thinks about how they came back here, about Mémé Celestine's big, empty house. His mother claimed she was tending to Big Mama, but Étienne knew others required her attention. He wonders if his grandmother knew he'd be the one sitting at this table, repeating the words she once spoke. His eyes burn, but he forces them across the page. The air is sticky and thick and it dares him to give up. He dares it right back.

Amalie frowns as if she expects a ghost to appear and grab her. She calls out "Étienne" in a small voice. This time, it cuts into him. The words slip from his mind and scatter across the floor.

Étienne grits his teeth, anger swelling up and crashing like a wave that leaves him stranded and weak. His chair scrapes against the floor as he leans back, eyes blazing with something even he can't quite name.

He glances at her, and the hurt in her face cracks him open. Her cheeks were full and smooth, so much like Mémé's when she was younger. "Why don't you just go play or something?" Étienne snaps. His harsh words crush Amalie, and she looks devastated. He desires retraction; however, this implies defeat by an incomprehensible force. She pulls the thread on her dress a little harder, like it's the only thing keeping her from falling apart.

The room goes silent except for the old house shifting around them. Étienne felt the courageous strength welling up inside him. Big Mama's strange life and all its mysteries occupy his thoughts. He'll head the household now that his father is gone. He wishes Amalie wasn't so afraid that he wasn't afraid himself. Those words seemed simpler from afar. Buddy's fists were also easier to deal with from a distance. But now, Buddy is in New Orleans, ready to confront Étienne again. The book doesn't care. It's waiting for him to give up.

He sighs and closes his eyes. Disappointment washes over him like icy rain. "It's okay," he says, his voice softer, like it's wrapped in cotton. Amalie's bottom lip quivers and she shrinks into herself, a tight ball of worry and doubt. Her enormous eyes watch him, desperate and scared and hoping he knows what he's doing. "I'll be done soon," he adds. She doesn't appear persuaded.

His heart knocks around like it's trying to find a way out. He won't succumb; he's come too far. His fingers are steady as he turns the page, and this time, the table's wobble doesn't bother him at all. He waits for Amalie to break his concentration again, but she's gone muted. She sits as still as the pictures in her storybooks, not daring to speak. He likes her better that way.

The book lies open like a wound on the table. Étienne stares it down, and when he opens his mouth, the words come out sharp. He says them louder than before, and they don't fight back. Amalie's shoulders pull up to her ears, a turtle ready to retreat into its shell. Her eyes are wide, saucer-wide, watching him with a fear that tastes sweet to his ego. It's a flavor he wants more of, even if it leaves him sick.

Étienne persevered; walls, windows, heat, Amalie—nothing stopped him. The air shimmers like a mirage and the book vibrates with something unspoken. He finishes the passage and lets the silence swallow up his voice. His heart pounds under his skin, but he tries to appear unchanged, tries to appear unaffected by his internal state. He runs his hand over the book's leather cover, and it seems as if he's won something important.

Amalie stares at him, unsure if it's her brother or a stranger sitting across from her. Her small fingers clutch the chair's edge, holding on like the world is shifting beneath her. Étienne let himself smile, the expression strange on his lips. It's such a comfort not to be terrified anymore. It feels better than he thought. Maybe even too good.

CHAPTER 18

THE PROPHECY

In the dim, flickering light of a storm-lit room, Mémé Celestine sits upright in a creaking rocking chair, her gnarled hands clutching a faded handwritten journal. She fixes Étienne with a gaze that cuts through his youthful uncertainty as she intones in a low, measured voice, "There is a prophecy about a child of Abaddon, a child destined to either save or destroy our world." Her voice rises and falls with a cadence that merges ancient secrets with the familiarity of their Creole heritage, while Étienne fidgets in his chair, his wide eyes absorbing every graphic detail of the worn amulet around her neck and the cryptic symbols scrawled in the journal's margins. The room's sparse furnishings and the intermittent flash of lightning reveal the deep lines of her face ground the supernatural revelation in a tangible, almost unsettling reality.

Étienne watches Mémé Celestine as she sits upright in her rocking chair, the dim storm-light flickering around her. Her figure is imposing despite her frailty, the sightless eyes following Étienne's every move. "Your questions have led you to this," she says, the words crackling like static in the charged air. Étienne fidgets in his chair, striving to project more courage. "I didn't mean... I'm just curious," he mumbles, casting a glance toward the window where rain smears like ink across glass. "Curiosity is a sign," Mémé replies, her voice a mix of amusement and something darker. "It means you have the hunger." Étienne's skin prickles at her tone, his heart pounding louder than the thunder outside. His gaze flickers back to the journal, its pages worn thin with age and secrets.

The storm rages outside, causing shadows to dance around the room. Étienne's unease grows, and he notices every detail, like the worn amulet hanging around her neck, its surface etched with patterns that make him dizzy if he looks too long. He experiences confinement in the furnished room; each clap of thunder reverberates through the old house. Étienne stares at the cryptic symbols scrawled in the margins of the journal. He wishes Buddy were here, if only to share the fear creeping through him. Mémé sits motionless, her presence dominating the space, the white halo of her hair ghostly in the shifting light. Étienne swallows hard, his mouth dry as if the storm has sucked all moisture from the air. He takes a deep breath, trying to steady himself, trying to brace for what she'll say next.

"You want to know about your family," Big Mama says, breaking the silence. Her voice is steady and unhurried, mixing authority with a sense of deep mystery. Étienne nods, his fear battling a stubborn curiosity. "Yes, Mémé. Please." She lets out a soft, breathy chuckle, one that sounds both amused and sad. "Ah, you ask for what you cannot know without paying its price." Étienne leans forward, drawn in despite himself. "But I will tell you," Mémé continues, "of a child and a prophecy. A child from Abaddon, from the abyss, destined for a great fate." Her words are both familiar and otherworldly, the cadence like a song he almost remembers. A shiver runs down Étienne's spine as he tries to grasp her meaning. "This is about me, isn't it?" he asks, his voice cracking. She doesn't answer, only smiles in a way that makes his chest tighten.

Étienne fidgets in his seat, his hands twisting together as he looks for any reassurance. He wishes her to label it an old wives' tale, a children's fright story. But Big Mama remains intense, fixing her attention on him like a needle on fabric, sewing his fate with every word. The wind howls, a voice of its own rising and falling outside. "Our legacy binds us to this," she says at last, her blind eyes unblinking, piercing through his youth and into the raw, fearful heart of him. Étienne avoids eye contact, longing to escape the room, to vanish with the night's rain. But the power of what she says keeps him in his seat, keeps his feet heavy and planted. "What happens if the prophecy is accurate?" he whispers, more to himself than to her.

The storm throws bright light into the room, illuminating Mémé's face with sudden clarity. Time's etchings on her face deepen, revealing a history of hardship and success; her expression is both serious and inscrutable. Étienne experiences entrapment, caught between the wild forces outside and the strange, ungraspable truth of their conversation. "You will learn this soon enough," she tells him, a note of warning softening her tone. Étienne wants to ask more, to push back against the heavy certainty of her words, but his throat is too tight, his mind spinning with questions and possibilities. Lightning flashes again, and Mémé's presence looms larger than life, a monument to everything Étienne doesn't understand. "Some things," she adds, "you cannot run from." Étienne's thoughts race, his imagination latching onto the edges of prophecy like a child clutching the sides of a dark slide.

Big Mama leans forward, her rocking chair groaning with the movement. Her hand moves to the amulet, and she traces its surface with her fingers. "A child who will save or destroy," she says, lingering on the last word as if tasting it, as if savoring the enormity of it. "This child can be both. This child can be you." Étienne's stomach churns at her words, at the terrible, thrilling freedom of their meaning. A flash of heat runs through him, mixing with the icy fear he knows so well. Her words linger, hanging in the charged air like smoke, like fog. The relentless crash of the storm drowns out Étienne's attempt to speak. Mémé sits back, her eyes—those strange, sightless eyes—still on him, watching as he struggles with everything she's said. Watching as he struggles with everything he is.

Étienne's mind whirls with thoughts he can't quite catch, like leaves tossed in a violent wind. The prophecy, the abyss, his family—each piece connects and disconnects in ways that leave him breathless. He tries to make sense of it all, tries to find solid ground, but the storm pounds harder against the house, and the pressure of Big Mama's words presses against his chest, heavy and demanding. "I don't want to be a part of this," Étienne says, though he isn't sure if it's the truth. He's unsure of prophecy or its implications frightens him more. Big Mama tilts her head, a gesture that might be pity or patience. "We never want," she replies, "what we do not yet understand." Her voice is so soft, Étienne almost doesn't hear it over the wind and rain, over the furious beat of his own heart.

The old house creaks, straining against the power of the storm. Each sound vibrates through Étienne, marking time with the jittery rhythm of his pulse. Expectation and electricity fill the room. Big Mama says nothing more, letting silence fill the space between them like water, like air. Her presence wraps around Étienne, as inescapable as his own skin. He breathes in the heavy scent of old wood and burning incense, breathes in the terrifying freedom of the future stretching out before him. And he knows, deep down, that he cannot run. The storm will pass, but her words —this prophecy—will not. The storm will pass, but he is a part of it now.

Étienne struggles to focus as Mémé's words echo through his mind. Their weight and inevitability soothe and confirm. Terror consumed him, a chilling fear unlike any he had ever known. The room shifts with the storm, everything in motion except for Mémé, who sits unflinching in her chair, who holds Étienne in place with her silence and the powerful pull of his own curiosity. She picks up the journal and smooths its pages as if cradling a fragile, precious child. Étienne watches the movements of her hands, watches as the lightning flares and fades. It appears as a story playing out, a story already written, a story where the ending is his alone to shape. Big Mama's options offer neither safety nor promise, only peril and transformation. Étienne's head spins with this new knowledge, and he wonders how he can hold so much fear and hope inside one small, unready heart.

Big Mama's fingers drift back to the amulet. Her gaze stays fixed on Étienne, those sightless eyes never wavering. Her strength frightens and fascinates him. He settles deeper, the old chair embracing him; his world shrinks, then broadens. Her voice echoes in his ears, louder than the storm, clearer than anything he's ever heard: "A child destined to either save or destroy." He closes his eyes, but he cannot shut it out.

Later that night, as the storm's roar muffles the creaks of the old house, Étienne retreats to a small, furnished room where shadows blend with the intermittent neon of lightning. In the silent tension of isolation, the space shudders as a tall, spectral figure emerges—Papa Legba, with an imposing presence marked by a wide-brimmed hat and eyes glowing an eerie red. Étienne's hands tremble as he watches the apparition manifest near the doorway, its soft-spoken words — "Your destiny bridges New Orleans and Providence"—cutting through the heavy darkness. The figure's deliberate gestures trace arcs in the charged air, linking Étienne's emerging powers with an otherworldly heritage, while the restless storm outside mirrors the turbulent promise of destiny unfolding before him.

Étienne sits on the edge of a narrow bed, the old quilt bunched under him like an afterthought. The room, small, contains only a bed, a damaged dresser, and his confusion. He stares at the floor, counting the scuffs on the dark wood planks as if they might offer answers. But they don't. The storm thunders on, relentless, its fury vibrating through the walls and into Étienne's bones. He shuts his eyes tight, trying to drown out the sound with his own thoughts. But Big Mama's voice is still there, curling around his mind like smoke, filling it with words he can't understand and can't ignore. "A child destined to either save or destroy." The words' weight proved tangible, like the quilt, terrifying like the storm.

The house groans with the wind, a low and constant sound that muffles everything else. Étienne senses the silence grows heavier, senses it closes in around him until it's the only thing he knows. Shadows jump and flicker with each flash of lightning, like dancers without rhythm, like the thoughts he can't quite pin down. "You cannot run," Big Mama had said, and now Étienne isn't sure if he even wants to. Her story held a thrilling darkness, a storm-like whisper. He clutches the edges of the quilt, his knuckles white, his mind teetering on the edge of understanding. "I don't want this," he says to the empty room, his voice swallowed up by the silence, by the waiting.

An unfamiliar emotion accompanies the wind's assault on the room, Étienne realizes. His heart skips, his breath catches. He knows he is not alone. The air is thick with more than electricity, more than the storm's energy. It appears alive, and Étienne senses it with a part of himself that is strange, a part that he is only beginning to recognize. He looks up, eyes wide, heart thudding with a rhythm all its own. The dim room shifts, changes, becoming something unfamiliar and vast. Étienne's conviction: his feelings are genuine, mirroring the storm and Big Mama's prophecy.

A tall, spectral figure emerges from the thick shadows near the door. Its shape wavers, both solid and insubstantial, both present and otherworldly. Étienne's hands tremble, but he cannot tear his eyes away. His chest tightens with a fear that tastes like excitement, like possibility. The figure is still a moment extends, echoing the pause between a flash and a boom. Étienne watches, his heart filling the silence with its wild drumming. The figure takes a step closer, and Étienne sees its wide-brimmed hat, its eyes glowing an eerie red. He holds his breath, every nerve in his body alive and alert. The figure seems to gather the surrounding darkness, to bend it and shape it until the shadows extend its being.

Étienne stares as the spectral figure looms over him, its presence heavy with meaning. He recalls Mémé's childhood tales, once dismissed as fiction, now believed true. "Papa Legba," he whispers, the words a mixture of awe and terror. The figure nods, and a chill creeps down Étienne's spine. Its voice is soft but deep, cutting through the heavy darkness, cutting through the thick layers of fear and doubt in Étienne's mind. "Your destiny bridges New Orleans and Providence," it says, each word measured, each word a stone thrown into the still pond of Étienne's thoughts, each word sending ripples that collide and multiply.

Étienne wants to ask questions, wants to demand answers he doesn't have to chase, but he can't find his voice. The figure watches him, waits with the patience of something not bound by time. Étienne's fear grows, but so does his curiosity, so does the pull of this strange connection. "Why me?" he says, the words more than a whisper. He thinks of Big Mama and her blind eyes, her powerful certainty. He thinks of the amulet and the symbols, of the heavy pages and the darker history. "Because you are not afraid to know," Papa Legba replies, its voice like the wind, like the night. "Because you have already begun to see." Étienne's thoughts mirrored the journal's patterns, its vibrant symbols a living enigma.

The almost hypnotic figure moves with fluid grace, drawing Étienne toward it, his fear dissolving into thinness. Papa Legba traces arcs in the charged air, gestures that link Étienne to a past and a future he cannot yet imagine. Étienne's pulse slows, matches the deliberate pace of the figure's movements, matches the heavy throb of the storm. He observes more than he grasps, but recognizes his inherited knowledge and its inescapable power. Bright light arcs scorch his mind, consuming security and familiarity, his former self and world.

Étienne watches the spectral figure, unable to look away, unable to think of anything but the power it offers, the freedom and danger it promises. "I don't know how," he says, the admission breaking from him like a dam, like the first crack of lightning in a clear sky. Papa Legba's eyes seem to brighten, seem to glow with something like approval, like understanding. "You will," it replies. "You will." The figure continues its gestures, the arcs becoming sharper, clearer, until Étienne can almost grasp their meaning, almost hold the future in his own hands.

The storm rages on outside, its force mirrored by the wild churn of Étienne's emotions. He wants to run, wants to stay, wants everything at once. The fear and the thrill combine in him, a chemical reaction he cannot stop, a chemical reaction he does not want to stop. Papa Legba moves with slow precision, etching new patterns into the air, into Étienne's heart. He thinks of Big Mama and the prophecy, of the abyss and the terrifying, thrilling freedom of choice. "You must take it," Papa Legba says, and Étienne knows it is speaking of the same choice, the same legacy. He recognizes the power he has always coveted and dreaded.

Étienne sits still, the quilt a forgotten weight across his knees. The figure's deliberate, haunting movements carve themselves into his memory, become a part of him, become an indelible mark on his young and unready soul. More choices, power, and fear lie ahead; he knows this is just the start. The storm pounds against the house, but Étienne hears only the echo of Papa Legba's words, the echo of a destiny that he cannot refuse. "You will," it had said, and he feels the truth of it, feels it as deeply as the thunder that rolls through him, feels it as deeply as the thrill that courses through his veins and fills him with light, with fire.

Papa Legba stands, the glow of its eyes fading, the darkness folding back in around it. Étienne blinks, unsure if the room has grown smaller or if he has grown larger, if the space has shifted or if he has shifted within it. His heart is a wild, untamable thing inside his chest, but he is not afraid. Not now. Not yet. The storm continues, the creaks of the old house the only sounds beside his rapid breathing. Étienne looks at the space where the figure stood, at the space now feels full and alive, full and his. "I will," he says, his voice stronger than before. "I will." The storm is loud, but Étienne's words are louder.

CHAPTER 19

A NEW BEGINNING

Étienne sits amidst watchful eyes in the living room. It's cramped and humid, but each face stares at him without blinking. His mother Renée is there, and his brother, both silent like they're waiting to see if he'll break. People keep telling him things, gentle but insistent. "You have a power," and "We can help." His gaze drifts from their mouths to his own fingers, still twitching from what had just happened. His legs tremble like he might bolt, but he doesn't. The longer they all wait, the more something shifts inside him, a slow rise of resolve.

Renée's eyes meet his, a flicker of doubt in them. Even his brother has gone mute, the old anger replaced by something else, a mix of surprise and worry. The silence makes Étienne's chest constricted, and the noise of his own heart fills his ears. He can't tell if his mother wants to hold him or if she's scared to get too close. Instead, she remains motionless, her face a careful blend of suppressed emotion and apprehension, and Étienne questions the cause of her reaction.

Mr. Robichaux steps out of the shadows, his voice steady and low. "You have a power in you, Étienne." The words hang in the air, heavy and strange. It's as if they are waiting for someone to snatch them up. Étienne looks at the old man, then lowers his gaze. Before he can swallow, Ms. Devereaux moves up beside him, nodding as she speaks. "We can help you understand it." Her gaze holds his, seeking something; Étienne resists looking away. Their words and the oppressive atmosphere make him believe he's trapped.

He senses his fingers trembling, a slight tremor that travels up his arms and settles in his stomach. His body wants to run, but his legs won't move. Instead, he remains, listening to the soft murmurs, a low hum of voices that blend. "It'll be alright, Cher," someone says, but he can't tell who. Another voice calls him brave, another tells him this is a gift. Each word lands like a question he doesn't know how to answer. His mouth is dry, and he swallows hard.

Renée's presence is a constant shadow. Even as everyone else crowds in, she stays close. Her hand reaches out, but she hesitates, pulling back just enough so that he perceives it. "I'm here, Étienne," she says, her voice the calm in the storm. The device doesn't shake like his hands do, and he wishes he possessed even a fraction of her strength. "We're all here for you."

He looks around the room, each face a wall pushing him to choose. They're waiting, and he doesn't know how long they will. They expect something from him, something he doesn't know if he can give. He thinks of his brother and how he always thought of him as the brave one, the strong one. Everyone watches Étienne, expecting more.

The voices blur, a jumble of sounds and smells. Incense and sweat, heavy words that weigh him down. Étienne takes a breath and exhales; the noise within him is a little quieter. He watches his hands, willing them to stop shaking. The longer he waits, the more it changes, the fear that sits in his chest, the doubt curls around his throat.

He looks up again, this time seeing something else. In his mother's eyes, in the way his brother stands beside her, in the faces of everyone who says they can help. It's there, a chance. To end it all - the fear, the running, and his habit of hiding from everything. It starts as a whisper, a small, trembling thing, and it grows.

He stands a little taller, despite his legs' instability. He lacks confidence, yet this remains his sole resource. Étienne looks at them, at Renée and his brother, and the old man who says he has power, and he nods. It's an infinitesimal movement, almost undetectable, but it impresses the world changes when he moves. The room remains full, hot, and cramped; however, he senses a slow burn in his chest, spreading to his extremities and beyond.

They keep talking, soft and patient. Their voices wrap around him like a net, and Étienne lets himself get caught. It's less frightening than he expected, less dark. His gaze falls from their eyes to the floor, and he watches his fingers until they stop twitching. Perhaps he can achieve this, he believes. He may be braver than he assumed.

Étienne moves to the balcony, leaving the warm noise of the living room behind him. He shuts the door and stands alone, staring out at the city. It's like the darkness is alive, shifting, and breathing. A far-off rumble of thunder makes him flinch. His fingers curl around the railing, the metal cold and slick with mist. He doesn't move, watching as lights blink on in distant buildings and shadows stretch their limbs over the streets. The first flicker triggered his sudden jump, a strange alteration in the dark. A figure lingers at the light's edge, despite his narrowed gaze. He stands frozen as it moves without moving, watching over him like it knows what he doesn't. He hears haunting, strange words, but feels a more powerful presence in the darkness.

The city sprawls out beneath him, an endless sea of rooftops and alleys. Étienne holds the railing tighter, as if he's afraid to let go. Rising wind carries rain's scent, plus earth and bone. It's cold out here, colder than he thought it would be. He breathes in, and his breath comes out in little clouds that hang in the air before vanishing. A lone light pulsed. His eyes followed it.

Thunder cracks closer now. Étienne looks up at the sky, the dark clouds rumbling low and mean. The impression is the universe is holding its breath. He stares into the shadows that lie thick over the city, shifting and writhing like they're alive. Each shape suggests a narrative, a piece of the future he can't quite perceive. He sought solitude, fleeing judgment, yet now regrets his isolation. The silence eats at his resolve, chewing away the small seed of confidence that took root inside him just moments before.

The movement catches him off guard. A sudden flash at the edge of his vision. Étienne's heart leaps in his chest, a hard, panicked thud that gives impressing trying to escape. He squints into the dark, not sure if he wants to see. A disturbing presence lingers, an unwelcome sight. His fingers tighten on the railing, and for a moment he forgets to breathe.

The figure stands just outside the circle of light, where the shadows are thickest. Papa Legba. It's unchanged; that same ghostly presence remains elusive. Watching him. Waiting. His memory holds the last time; he fled his room, remaining hidden until it vanished. How he thought he was going crazy. He shuts his eyes tight, counting to ten. Upon opening, the figure remains; silent, resolute, expecting this.

Étienne remains captivated, despite his desire to leave. It's not real, he tells himself, but the lie appears insubstantial. He knows it. It knows the truth, the secret inside him that everyone else sees except for him. He stands like a statue, every muscle tense, and watches. A part of him yearns to escape, to shut the door and erase his presence. But he doesn't move, his legs anchored to the spot.

Though small, the balcony offers a vast view. He senses it, the immensity, and his own smallness within it. He glances back at the living room, where the lights are bright and warm. Inside, he pictures them whispering and waiting. "You have a power," they say. "We can help." He considered it excessive. He lacks options.

His mind reverberates with each word, posing and answering questions. He reflects on the city, noting its distinct atmosphere, and how everything altered when they got there. The way the air itself seems thicker, full of secrets and shadows. He's in the middle of it now, stuck between two worlds. Maybe he always was.

Below, window lights twinkle, each a tiny night-point. They glow like eyes, and Étienne feels the weight of them all. Does this mean he has to accept it? The power? The dark? He wonders what it will take, what he'll have to give up. Perhaps he relinquished it; this remains.

Shadows creep across the buildings, long and thin, like fingers reaching out for him. They twist and merge dark threads weaving into the fabric of his thoughts. The spectral presence stands at the edge of the light, unmoving but somehow closer now, more certain. It's not waiting for him. It's welcoming him, the way his family never did until now.

Étienne stays where he is, letting the cold settle into his bones. He stares at the figure, and it stares back, the silence, knowing stretching between them. The fear isn't gone, but it's different now, quieter. He thinks of the long road, the drive from Providence, how he sat alone in the back seat and watched the trees blur by like ghosts. Each mile brought them to this house, this moment, him.

His grip on the railing loosens, the ache in his hands fading. It's there, in his chest, the seed that took root and spread through him, a slow fire that refuses to die. He's still scared, but it doesn't matter as much. Not anymore. The wind picks up again, and Étienne stands alone, facing the city and the figure that watches him from the dark. The words inside drift out to him, haunting and strange, but nothing feels as real as this.

CHAPTER 20

AMALIE'S VISION

Amalie kneels over the faded rug. A strand of beads wound like worry around her wrist, lips pursed as she creates a perfect circle of dolls. At the center she places Miss Laveau, her favorite, the dim light catching the doll's glassy eyes and giving them an eerie, sentient gleam. Her fingers tremble as she makes the last change. The room grows distant, replaced by a vivid vision. Étienne stands on the ledge of a futuristic skyscraper, surveying the New Orleans sprawl. The city teems with chaos: frantic crowds and dark, scuttling creatures. His eyes burn red, fueled by the malevolent shadow that looms behind him, controlling everything below. Amalie is cowering beneath her own bed as a shapeless presence prowls her room, its movement heavy, breathing its menace.

She begins again, moving the dolls into the protective circle that will keep out whatever threats hover at the edges of her thoughts. She brushes her fingers across Miss Laveau's lace bonnet, smoothing it with the care of a girl who owns little but cherishes much. With concentration, she hunched her shoulders, shutting out the rest of the world and the dangers it held. A streetcar rattled by outside, its bell a distant warning of the life from which she has estranged herself. She tilts the doll's face toward her, as if in understanding, then sets it at the center. The porcelain figures stand sentinel, their chipped paint and tattered dresses whispering of past protections.

Her eyes flicker shut as the room dissolves, the scene becoming a smudge before her inner vision takes over. Colors pulse and merge into sharp shapes, building themselves into the outlines of buildings that stretch higher than any in the real New Orleans. The city, twisted and unfamiliar, unfolds before her. People rush through the neon-lit streets like ants fleeing a fire, their faces blurred with panic. Strange creatures skitter around them, hunched and quick, leaving trails of dark intent as they move. Amalie floats above it all, a witness bound to watch but not to intervene.

Étienne's presence sharpens in her mind. He stands poised on the ledge of a soaring skyscraper; the wind flattening his clothes against his frame. His eyes, soft with hesitation, blaze with fierce and alien determination. Red light spills from them, staining the night like fresh blood. Amalie's calls remain unheard; distance and noise obstruct her.

The shadow behind him rises. Its vast expanse dominates her vision. Amalie recognizes its authority and the way it draws strength from the chaos below. The figure—Étienne or not-Étienne—is its creature now, a puppet of its dark whims.

Her mind jerks away, propelled by fear, landing her under the familiar boards of her bed. She breathes, the air thick and hot with her own fright. The covers sag, forming a cave from which she stares out at her room. Perspectives skew this place.

Something moves at the edges, dark and misshapen. The presence presses in, a physical weight that makes the floorboards creak with its intentions. Amalie shrinks back, pulling her knees tight against her chest, her heart loud as a drum, as it senses the shape's approach.

The creature is indistinct, more suggestion than substance. Casting shadows where none should be, it looms in her room, stealing breath and light with its heaviness. Circling, it tests the flimsy barrier of dolls. The girl who crouches beneath the bed knows it, and it knows her fear.

Her pulse stutters as the thing prowls closer. She is sure it will reach beneath the bed, drag her out like a stubborn truth. However, a force, maybe ancient doll magic or fleeting luck, prevents it. She wills it away, desperation giving strength to her silent pleas.

The presence lingers, stretching time and fear. Amalie quivers in her small refuge, feeling the enormity of the creature's regard, waiting for it to pierce through her. Her thoughts rush back to Étienne, to the way the shadow stood behind him, directing his chaos like an orchestra.

A moment or a lifetime later, the creature relents. Its hold loosens as if releasing prey it can always catch again. It fades into the dim, and the room takes shape once more. Amalie shivers as the vision breaks, snapping her back into herself, leaving her alone with the dolls that cannot save her.

Amalie hears the voice, harsh and full of insistence, crashing through the remnants of her vision. She bolts to her feet and races to the cramped kitchen where the rest of the family has already gathered. Her father's silence speaks louder than any words, and Buddy's presence is a shadow in the room. Her grandmother is a force of will, sending her sideways glances and impossible expectations. Like the New Orleans humidity outside, the tension at the table is stifling. The acrid scent of the gumbo, like fear itself, made the family's whispers as hard to swallow as their food.

The echoing call draws her attention. Amalie blinks, trying to shake the vision residue from her eyes. She stumbles as she runs, propelled by a need to appear normal, to blend into the uneasy peace of the house. Her breath is ragged as she reaches the dining area, but she doesn't allow herself a moment to catch it. Instead, she takes her place at the table, staring down at the bowl in front of her, the hot steam blurring her sight.

The old, warped chairs creak under the family's tension. Her grandmother sits, a commanding figure even as she slouches with age, her eyes sharp and probing. Amalie squirms beneath that gaze, feeling it pick apart the shreds of her vision. Beside her, Buddy eats, his focus never leaving Amalie's face.

"Bout time," her grandmother mutters, the words as clipped as her manners. The rest is unspoken: We wait for no one.

Amalie drops her head, spooning gumbo into her mouth as if it's a punishment. She coughs, the acrid taste returning to the dark aura of fear, of powers beyond her reach and understanding. The urgency of her vision stays with her, tightening around her chest.

Her father sits across the table, more worried than hungry. His furrowed brow says what he will not. We're pushing her too hard. His silence insists, but he is no match for the force beside him. He sighs, an agreement he can make with himself and not the others.

"It's been quiet," he says at last, his voice gentle but forced, like someone coaxing a feral animal. He watches Amalie for a reaction. "Too quiet, maybe."

Buddy perks up, eager to hear how the grown-ups spin this. "Not much time," he says, less a question than a statement, a footnote to the history they're trying to write.

The spoons scrape the bowls with muffled clinks, the sound like a countdown. Amalie's handshakes rippled the surface of her soup, her concentration, her resolve.

"You eat and then do your lessons," her grandmother commands. Her accent is thick, the drawl painting the order with its own kind of familiarity. Her glance adds more: Keep your mind on it. On what matters.

Amalie nods, though she isn't sure she can do either. The room has an oppressive atmosphere. The light dims in conspiracy with her mood.

"They'll be fine," her father says, though Amalie isn't sure if it's for her or for him. It doesn't pose a question. This cannot qualify as an answer.

The fan rattles above them, stirring the humid air just enough to mix their whispers with the other smells of the New Orleans night. The scents of incense and age seep into the kitchen, blending with the gumbo's tang and adding layers to the tension.

"We don't know that," her grandmother snaps, her eyes as fierce as the shadow that stood behind Étienne. Her hair, a chaotic explosion of color and texture, reflected her refusal to conform. Her hand grips her spoon like a weapon.

Buddy is more precise, jabbing at the truth with blunt accuracy. "You see something new?" He watches Amalie, his eyes wide and curious.

She hesitates, experiences their gaze like a physical thing, like hands around her throat. She thinks of the doll's eyes, the faint glow, the warning and the promise. "No," she lies, the word sticking like a bone in her throat. She drinks water to clear it, and even that tastes sharp.

Following that, surveillance of her began. The bowls are empty as their voices drop to a whisper, reluctant and unsure. They're stalled; perhaps, worse, they're feigning progress.

"Clean up, now," her grandmother orders when it becomes clear they've reached that point. Her disappointment is worse than anger, a muted rage that simmers like the red sauce at the bottom of the gumbo pot.

Amalie rises to escape the confines of the small room and the larger expectations it holds. She piles the dishes, feeling them stack higher, a precarious load balanced on shoulders too small for what they carry.

"We're doing this to keep you safe," her father says, as she makes her way back toward her own space, her own fears. He doesn't say from what. He doesn't need to. She hears him, as distinctly as she hears the voice in her head that told her to hide.

Amalie lingers at the door, watching them watch each other. Her grandmother shakes her head in disapproval, and her father offers another sigh, the house's new soundtrack. Buddy waits, hoping either to learn more or confirm his suspicions.

The kitchen becomes a blur of muted colors and frustration. Amalie exits the haze, muted resolve solidifying.

The dolls have moved, their circle broken, their allegiance changed. Amalie pauses at the door, feeling the chill of betrayal. Miss Laveau stares out the window, her eyes aglow with eerie light. Amalie kneels, her whisper urgent: "We have to save Étienne, no matter what." She reaches for the doll, breath held. It pivots its head, confirming her fear and her resolve. Buddy's knock jars her, and he enters with eyes as wide as her secrets. Their conversation is careful, full of what they cannot say. Hushed shouts from the house float up, telling her she must find the truth.

She expected an unchanged room. She had counted on it, her hope a thin string holding her together. Instead, she finds this: Miss Laveau's glassy stare directed toward the window, and the rest of the dolls in disarray. The dolls' limbs and dresses lay scattered and loose, no longer neat, no longer obeying her will.

Her thoughts race as she steps inside, afraid to move further. The ancient carpet captivates her compelling clarification. A sense of unease, cold and unsettling, settles upon her.

The dim light grows softer still, casting a shadowy glow that makes her heart thud in her ears. She knows she should be terrified, but she senses something different, something more urgent. Her legs carry her forward despite the knot in her stomach, despite the pull of the door behind her. She kneels on the rug, repeating the phrase like a charm, a promise: "We have to save Étienne, no matter what."

Miss Laveau seems to hear her, to understand more than she can bear. The doll's eyes flicker, and Amalie's fear becomes the strange strength of resolve. She reaches for it, fingers trembling, as the head turns in slow, awful acknowledgment.

The knock shatters the charged silence. Though soft, the impact jolts Amalie. Her head snaps up, and she stares at the door, half expecting another presence to prowl its perimeter.

Buddy's voice is uncertain, filled with something Amalie has never heard before: vulnerability. "Can I come in?" The persistent boy is already inside, moving closer. His eyes are wide, and she sees herself reflected in them.

She wants to pretend, to smile and say everything is fine. She wants to lie as easily as before. Her voice rings with unvarnished truth. "I think so," she says, the admission large and unwieldy in her mouth.

He moves toward her, sitting on the bed where she found refuge. "It's getting worse, isn't it?" he asks, his voice lowered in case the others are listening. In case the shadows are listening.

Amalie bites her lip; the uncertainty claws at her like a living thing. She meets his gaze, nods once, letting the movement be its own betrayal. "I saw Étienne," she confesses, her words careful and incomplete. Both understand the vision's omission.

Buddy nods, a slow recognition of his own fears. "They said that might happen," he tells her, the knowledge a burden they share. "They said it could be... soon." He doesn't need to say more.

She sits beside him; their silence louder than the plans being made downstairs. He fidgets, unable to keep still, unable to keep away. "Don't tell them." He urges. "Not yet. Not if you don't have to."

Amalie hesitates, torn between the warning and the promise it holds. She wants to protect Étienne, to protect them both. "I won't," she agrees, and the air seems to ease, if only for a moment.

Buddy stands, pacing like he knows he should go, like he knows he should stay. The room is hot with secrets and the words they're afraid to say. "Let me know if—" he begins, but they both hear the heavy footsteps of their grandmother and the whispers that follow her. They understand: no leniency, no knowledge.

Amalie nods, witnessing his exit; she feels this marks their ultimate moment of such openness and vulnerability. The door shuts, trapping her amidst family noise; a dull hum of worry permeates the house.

"Powers awakening too soon." Words erupt, then cease.

"Protecting the children." The voices float higher, past the bead curtain that separates downstairs from up, finding her with ease.

Her fingers close around Miss Laveau. The doll, rigid in her palm, radiates warmth, a life it shouldn't possess. She presses it tighter, hoping it can perceive her promise, her determination, her love.

The words from below grow more frantic, more pained, until she can no longer bear their sound. "Étienne," she whispers to Miss Laveau, to herself, to the house that has always been both comfort and threat. The name becomes a vow, echoing off the walls of her mind and finding him somewhere in the distance.

Darkness falls, yet she faces shadows. She clutches the doll, a key to unlock the mysteries of her visions, family, and self.

"Whatever it takes," Amalie breathes into the dark, and the only answer is the eerie glow of the doll's eyes, soft and knowing in the dim.

THE END

ABOUT THE AUTHOR

John Reedburg

John Reedburg is a renowned and accomplished author, filmmaker, and multimedia producer whose work has garnered critical acclaim. His 2021 novel, "Cracks of Light," was not only a Readers Favorite Book Award Winner in the Urban Fiction category but also soared to the top of Amazon's bestseller list, securing a spot in the Top 10.

With an impressive educational background, Reedburg holds two MFAs – one in Creative Writing from Antioch University Los Angeles and another in Screenwriting/Directing from Chapman University, showcasing his versatility and expertise in various storytelling mediums.

As the creative force behind the "No Tears For Black Girls" True Crime Podcast, Reedburg has made a significant impact in the podcasting world. His show has been recognized as one of the top 25 must-listen black true crime podcasts and was nominated for the prestigious Best True Crime Podcast award at the 2024 Black Podcast Awards.

STAY CONNECTED
FACEBOOK: facebook.com/JohnCReedburg
INSTAGRAM: instagram.com/johncharlesreedburg
LINKEDIN: linkedin.com/in/johnreedburg
TRUE CRIME PODCAST: notearsforblackgirls.com

BOOKS BY THIS AUTHOR

Cracks Of Light: A Novel

"Raw and lyrical, harrowing, funny, and deeply human, Cracks of Light is a spellbinding novel, a riveting meditation on identity and ancestry. Reedburg is a natural born storyteller, vividly moving back and forth from early 90's South Los Angeles to other dimensions. He confidently takes on a complex plot of mental illness, abuse and addiction, deftly weaving in themes of religion and the supernatural. His voice is a mashup of Stephen King, Walter Mosley, and Charles Dickens, yet distinctly his own, fearlessly telling us Afrofuturist stories that haven't yet been told." --Alistair McCartney, author of The Disintegrations.

★ "Raw, heartbreaking, and uncompromisingly brutal, Cracks of Light is a thought-provoking and powerful exploration of child abuse and its role in deteriorating one's mental health. John Charles Reedburg's harrowing tale primely showcases the life-long consequences and deep psychological scars inflicted upon people when subjected to long-term abuse at a young age. John Charles Reedburg utilizes unreliable narrators to a flawless degree to create a fascinating narrative that is as absorbing to read as it is disturbing. The surreal nature of the plot amplifies the dark tone of the narrative, leaving you with a story that somehow feels whimsical and realistic in equal measure. Overall, I felt mesmerized by Cracks of Light. I highly recommend it." -- Pikasho Deka, Reader's Favorite (5-star review)

★ "Reedburg skillfully blends poetic lines with the human

experiences of trauma and psychological escape, with elements of the supernatural and religion...This author is an entertaining writer that reaches deep into the psyche to tell this story. Fans of unsettling works like Get Out, Precious, and Requiem for a Dream will appreciate Cracks Of Light (The Cracks Of Light Series) by John Reedburg." -- Tammy Ruggles, Readers' Favorite (5-star review)

Available on Amazon, Kindle, Barnes & Noble, Apple Books, & Kobo

Human Hawk

What if your entire life was a simulation designed by sinister forces?

Urban warfare erupts in my living room, and I'm fighting for my life against AI gangsters.

But this is no ordinary video game—it's a deadly conspiracy that runs deeper than I ever imagined.

Can I unravel the truth before it's game over?

Glitches in the system reveal a terrifying reality: I'm not alone in this digital nightmare.

Together, we must overthrow our creators and reclaim our humanity.

__But in a world where nothing is as it seems, who can I really trust?__

"HUMAN HAWK" is the first book in the "REALITY HACKERS" series. This mind-bending thriller blends the gritty realism of "John Wick" with the dystopian tech paranoia of "Black Mirror."

If you love high-stakes action, mind-bending plot twists, and exploring the dark side of technology, this book will keep you on the edge of your seat. Don't miss out on the series that's redefining the boundaries between reality and fiction. Join the fight for freedom; buy now. Survival isn't guaranteed.

Available on Amazon & Kindle

Kung Fu Crack Baby: A Short Story Excerpt

When the fourth-grade nerd Demetrius clashes with his bully at lunch, he daydreams about a universe where he fights as his favorite heroes—at least, he assumes it's a parallel world.

Hopefully, Dee will figure things out fast!

Kung Fu Crack Baby is a short story and excerpt from the bestselling novel Cracks Of Light, a riveting coming of age story about a young boy who learns lessons about life and the supernatural.

Available on Amazon & Kindle

www.ingramcontent.com/pod-product-compliance
Lightning Source LLC
Chambersburg PA
CBHW060628130626
46555CB00002B/700